# Fonseca

ALSO BY JESSICA FRANCIS KANE

*Bending Heaven*
*The Report*
*This Close*
*Rules for Visiting*

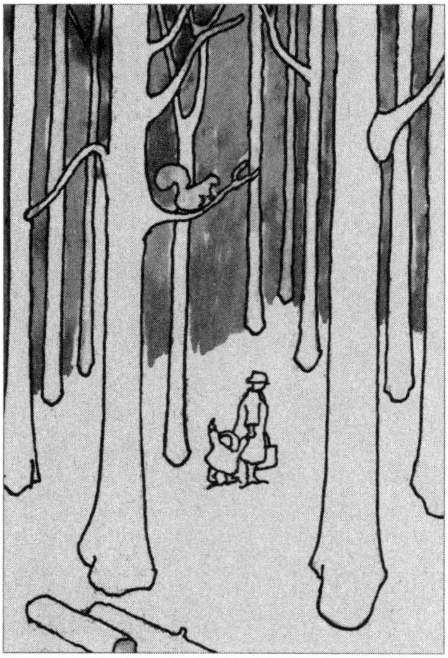

# Fonseca

*A Novel*

JESSICA FRANCIS KANE

Penguin Press ·· New York ·· 2025

PENGUIN PRESS
An imprint of Penguin Random House LLC
1745 Broadway, New York, NY 10019
penguinrandomhouse.com

Copyright © 2025 by Jessica Francis Kane

Penguin Random House values and supports copyright.
Copyright fuels creativity, encourages diverse voices, promotes free speech, and creates a vibrant culture. Thank you for buying an authorized edition of this book and for complying with copyright laws by not reproducing, scanning, or distributing any part of it in any form without permission. You are supporting writers and allowing Penguin Random House to continue to publish books for every reader. Please note that no part of this book may be used or reproduced in any manner for the purpose of training artificial intelligence technologies or systems.

PP colophon is a registered trademark of Penguin Random House LLC.

Frontmatter and backmatter illustrations by Penelope Fitzgerald, courtesy of Christina Dooley and Edmund Valpy Fitzgerald

Letters published courtesy of Christina Dooley and Edmund Valpy Fitzgerald

Set in Adobe Caslon Pro
*Designed by Christina Nguyen*

LIBRARY OF CONGRESS CATALOGING-IN-PUBLICATION DATA
Names: Kane, Jessica Francis, 1971– author.
Title: Fonseca : a novel / Jessica Francis Kane.
Description: New York : Penguin Press, 2025.
Identifiers: LCCN 2024042027 (print) | LCCN 2024042028 (ebook) |
ISBN 9780593298855 (hardcover) | ISBN 9780593298862 (ebook)
Subjects: LCGFT: Novels.
Classification: LCC PS3611.A543 F66 2025 (print) |
LCC PS3611.A543 (ebook) | DDC 813/.6 23/eng/20240906—dcundefined
LC record available at https://lccn.loc.gov/2024042027
LC ebook record available at https://lccn.loc.gov/2024042028

Printed in the United States of America
1st Printing

The authorized representative in the EU for product safety and compliance is Penguin Random House Ireland, Morrison Chambers, 32 Nassau Street, Dublin D02 YH68, Ireland, https://eu-contact.penguin.ie.

*For Mitchell, who always
knew what Fonseca meant*

Unfortunate are the adventures
which are never narrated.

—Penelope Fitzgerald

# NOVEMBER

## ·· *Day of the Dead* ··

In 1952 November 2 fell on a Sunday, and that afternoon a mother and son stood in front of the Delaney house in Fonseca, Mexico, poised to knock. They had traveled a long way, were quite stunned, mainly from the last leg of their journey through the American South, and now it was late afternoon the day after the day they were supposed to have arrived. The season was warm, and in the square behind them people were wearing calaveras and the air smelled of smoke and marigolds. In the distance and also quite nearby they heard the pop and spray of fireworks. A band was playing in the square, the music brassy and bright, punctuated by shouts. It was all very disconcerting, and even though he didn't know who or what was behind the door, the boy wanted to go inside. In all his six years, he had never entered a house that did not have someone making or about to make tea. But his mother would not knock.

"This isn't a holiday," Valpy said, turning to sit down on the front step. A young woman passed chewing a large sugar calavera with the name Pedro across the forehead. She was sobbing and laughing at the same time.

Penelope sat down next to him. "How can you tell?"

"I've never had new clothes for a holiday before."

"That's not true. What about your bathing costume last summer?"

He didn't say anything. They both knew bathing costumes didn't count.

"And this is a very strange house." The gray stone with wood shutters in the French style was at odds with all the buildings around it, every one stucco in the colors of sunset. The house stood right up against the pavement, three gabled sections around a shallow front courtyard. Five steps led up from the front wall to what looked like the door of a castle keep, old oak with iron bolts and bars. Above and to the left was a heavy, rounded balcony that reminded Penelope of a pulpit. There were several tall chimneys, two dormers, and a number of mullioned windows in various sizes, all shuttered. Old, twisted pecan trees on the street further darkened the front.

"Yes, but there's nothing to be afraid of," Penelope said.

This was an error. Valpy had not said he was afraid, and now Penelope saw that he was looking at the trees and the heavy little balcony and wondering if he should be. "We were invited," she reminded him quickly.

"But why were we invited?"

"The Delaneys are old friends."

"But why do they want to see us?"

Later, when the house in Southwold was emptied, and even

later, when their houseboat *Grace* went down, Penelope would remember this moment on the step of the house in Fonseca. Everyone has a point to which the mind reverts naturally when it is left on its own. This was hers.

"It's hard to explain," she said.

This was not untrue. The Delaneys, two wealthy old women, had written to Penelope more than half a year ago to say they were alone in the world, all their relations in Ireland were gone, and because of some distant friendship between their families, they hoped to meet Valpy. Indeed, if Penelope had understood their letters correctly, they suggested they might leave him all their money. This possibility was tantalizing for a number of very pressing reasons. She stood and knocked quickly, pecan shells cracking underfoot.

"Dios mío, two of you!" the housekeeper exclaimed, pulling open the heavy door. "Have you just come from the bus?" She was about fifty, with wide, bare arms under a red apron. Her dark hair was pulled into a middle part, the length of it braided and wound on top of her head, a yellow marigold tucked behind one ear, heavy cheeks flushed under blue eyes. Penelope, who was not particularly tall, towered over her.

Valpy bravely cleared his throat. "Yes, but first we were on the *Queen Mary*, then the bus. It was a long and terrible ride. Actually, first we were on a train, but that wasn't part of the adventure because it was still in England."

"That sounds right. Very few adventures begin and end in England. Where was the boat's port of call?"

"New York," Valpy answered.

"Good. One of you can take the bus back there." She took Valpy's hand, suggesting Penelope would be the one returning.

Penelope countered with a hand to Valpy's shoulder. "But I notified Doña Elena that we were both coming."

"I don't remember that letter."

"Yet you know it *was* a letter."

"How else would you have told her?"

"I might have sent a telegram. Or phoned."

The housekeeper narrowed her eyes. "Too expensive." She adjusted the marigold behind her ear. "We expected you yesterday."

"I'm sorry. We were delayed in San Antonio."

"That was the terrible part," Valpy said.

The housekeeper nodded as if she understood, but how could she have known what happened?

The three stood on the doorstep, seemingly at an impasse. Finally Penelope said, "This is ridiculous! He's only six years old. He never could have made this journey alone."

"Why?" the housekeeper said, scrutinizing Valpy. "Is there something wrong with him?"

Valpy shook his head.

"Of course not," Penelope said. "But it would be a very long journey for so young a child."

"How far is it?"

Valpy knew the exact mileage from the front door of their house, Chestnut Lodge, Hampstead, London, to the doorstep where they were standing in Zona Centro, Fonseca, Mexico.

"That is far," the housekeeper said. "He should be with his mother."

Penelope was relieved. "Now we agree. I am his mother."

The housekeeper sighed. She stepped backward, pulling the door with her. "I am Chela. Welcome to Mirando."

Penelope didn't move. "I thought this was the Delaney house?"

"Yes, yes, come in."

It was an inauspicious, topsy-turvy start, and Penelope never forgot it.

THE LARGE, WOOD-PANELED front hall was decorated for the holiday with potted marigolds lining both sides of the wide center staircase. These were mostly orange, orange threaded with darker orange, and a few yellow here and there. They must have just been watered, for the smell of damp soil filled the hall. Convivial sounds came from the floor above, and there was opera playing somewhere.

"Are you having a party?" Valpy looked hopeful for the first time since they'd knocked.

"No," Chela said. "Those people are here just like you. The Doñas are in the cemetery. Leave your trunk for Jesús." Chela looked at Valpy and then spelled for his benefit. "That's J-E-S-U-S. He will bring it up."

Penelope was troubled by some of this information and Valpy was wide-eyed, but there was no time for questions. Chela moved fast for one so round around the middle. At the top of the staircase, she turned left, then right to the bottom of a smaller staircase. She took this to the third floor and turned right again down a tiled hall, where she stopped in front of a door that looked like it might have once been painted blue.

"Come down when you're ready," she said, not in the least out of breath, "but not before five o'clock. Mr. Azuela will be finished with his report by then. The washroom is down the hall. You'll be sharing with the Tuttles. For some reason they like to say their room faces the sea, but it is six hundred kilometers to the east. Your room faces the mountains, the beautiful Sierra Madre. But don't be fooled. They are farther than they seem."

"Tuttles?" Penelope said.

"An organist and his wife from Ireland. Penniless. No one can remember how long they've been here."

"Do they also have a son?" She had not expected competition.

Chela laughed. "Not that I've seen!" She looked more seriously at Valpy. "Why? Are you worried about being lonely? There is plenty to do at Mirando. We have a garden and chickens, and a flock of mourning doves roosts on the roof. There is also a cat, Pax. He does what he likes and goes where he pleases."

"Thank you," Penelope said. "I'm sure we'll be fine."

"We'll see." Chela opened the once-blue door with a key and ushered them in. "Laundry is on Mondays, bedclothes every other week." She closed the door and left them, the peppery scent of marigolds lingering behind her.

Valpy looked as if he were about to cry. "Are Mr. and Mrs. Tuttle old friends too?"

"I'm sure they are," Penelope said.

The room, up under the eaves of Mirando, had a sloped ceiling and a set of mullioned windows that did indeed, when Penelope opened the shutters, look over rooftops toward the blue-tinged mountains. There was a double bed with a blue quilt, a small desk without a chair, and a wardrobe in the back left corner. To the right was a chaise upholstered in dark red velvet that felt large for the room, but would do nicely as a second bed. There was a glazed jug and basin under a shelf and mirror on the wall, a little wooden bench, and a small electric fan. The room was clean and tidy though the air was still. Penelope turned on the fan.

"Is Jesús going to bring the trunk? Is that really what's going to happen?"

Penelope explained that it was probably not an uncommon name in Spanish.

"We are very far from home," Valpy said.

She was prepared for this and gave him the best advice she had based on her own experience being sent away to school at eight. The words came out with a ferocity that startled them both.

"Homesickness is a real illness, Valpy. Don't believe anyone who tells you it isn't."

Dear ——

I was so interested in your letter with its description of how you came to know my mother's work. Interested and also reassured because I can see that you understand her and her life as far as one can ever know or understand other people's lives. I often wonder why I didn't ask her more about herself and decisions she made and then I remember that she always evaded questions and never gave direct or detailed answers.

My brother Valpy lives in a remote mountain village in Spain most of the year though he also has a small town house in Oxford where he was a professor. He would like to get in touch to share his memories of the 1952 trip to Mexico (to Saltillo, not "Fonseca").

Thank you for telling us about Hopper. His Mexican paintings are so atmospheric and you can feel the heat. I think the dividing line between fiction and fact is quite blurred in her biographies and her novels so you push on.

With all best wishes,
Tina

## *Greed?*

Doña Elena's first letter arrived at Chestnut Lodge in the spring. She introduced herself as a family friend who, in spite of the recent nationalization, lived comfortably off the proceeds of her family's silver mine. She and her sister-in-law, Anita, had lived in Fonseca since they were girls. Would Penelope and her family—they believed she had a son?—like to come for a visit?

Penelope had no memory of friends named Delaney. Nor did Desmond, whose family was Irish. He said it was a lark. They'd never hear from this person again.

But a few days later, a second letter arrived, this one from Doña Anita, though the handwriting looked similar. The plan it suggested was more detailed. It was, specifically, Valpy they were interested in. Could they send him? To put it plainly—and Doña Anita did, Penelope believed—they were in need of an heir.

"Could Doña Anita have been drinking?" Penelope said. The

hand was wobbly and grew larger and looser as it progressed down the page. "What do you think?"

Desmond shook his head.

Penelope wrote back. Of course she did. Anyone who has ever been in need of money will understand this. She and Desmond were coeditors of a struggling literary journal, had just made an ill-advised move to a larger house, and had two children under six. A legacy of any kind would be a godsend, and she did not use that word lightly. If their financial situation didn't improve, they would have to leave London, a thought she couldn't abide.

In her return letter she asked if the Doñas could just perhaps remind her of the connection between their families? She also mentioned that Valpy, though intelligent, steady, and serious of manner, was only six years old.

The response took some weeks, and when it arrived revealed the Doñas had indeed thought Valpy was older. Nevertheless, they were delighted to learn he was still a boy. He could attend school with the nuns at the Church of San Esteban near their house.

Desmond was alarmed. "Now he is enrolling in school?" But he pulled out the atlas and found the town on the map.

It seemed the family connection was on Penelope's mother's side. Elena's mother, Helen O'Sullivan, had been great friends with Penelope's grandmother, Agnes Smith. Where or how this could have been they did not say, but the Doñas closed again—Penelope remained certain of it—with an explicit invitation to stay with them in Fonseca. They should come at their earliest convenience, the letter said. The Doñas wished to settle the question of their estate soon.

"This is madness," Desmond said.

"It might be madness not to try," said Penelope. She knew the recent circulation numbers for *World Review* better than he did, and she knew how expensive the move to Chestnut Lodge had been, engineered in part to give them more room for entertaining for the journal. She'd overspent on some of the decorating, and their bank account was perilously low. She dreamed of money every night. In fact, Penelope's worries so often concerned money it was not uncommon for her thoughts to take the form of an interview with a bank manager.

"You should go," the bank manager told her.

"But how?" she asked. He often told her what she should do, but not how she should do it.

"A legacy would solve a lot of problems."

"I'm not confused about that," she snapped.

In August, Penelope and Desmond celebrated two years at the journal, but the occasion promised little of the excitement they'd felt originally when they acquired Salinger's "For Esmé—with Love and Squalor" for their first issue. Their tenth wedding anniversary was the same month. For the issue, they ran the second and final part of a feature on Spanish painted sculpture and a short story by Muriel Spark. For the anniversary, they walked with Valpy and Tina on Hampstead Heath, then came back to Chestnut Lodge for a picnic in the garden. It was lovely weather, wholly different from the overcast day of their wedding. Wedding rain was supposed to be a harbinger of luck, and she wouldn't have minded it. But it had not actually rained, only threatened, and their luck, then as now, remained in low supply.

They'd been at Oxford at the same time, Desmond at Magdalen reading history, Penelope at Somerville reading English. They'd known some of the same people; Penelope heard stories of two Irish brothers who liked to climb roofs and drink beer, but she was ambitious and academic, and their groups did not mingle. They met later, at a party in London, 1940 or '41; she told people she could never remember. But she did, it was just such a silly story. In a warm and crowded room, she'd bumped into him and said sorry. He turned, saw her, and said, "I'm not." By then she'd been in love, had had at least five suitors, declined two proposals, and was planning to make it through the war without getting married. But she was Desmond's first love. He was charming, funny, well traveled, and well read. She was working at the BBC, writing book and film reviews for *Punch*, and everyone she introduced him to said he was dashing. He was. Tall and long-legged and overwhelmingly handsome. They were engaged by May 1942, married in August.

Then, February 1943. The first of her three extraordinary uncles, Dillwyn Knox, died, just awarded the CMG for his cryptanalysis work at Bletchley. The next day Desmond sailed to North Africa with the First Battalion of the Irish Guards. The Guards led the landings at Anzio and fought their way up to the siege of Monte Cassino, enduring some of the worst fighting of the war. Desmond was awarded the Military Cross for "the highest degree of personal courage," but he returned in 1945 utterly changed. For months he woke in the night shouting; he could never again bear fireworks.

He finished his legal training and was called to the Bar, but he was miserable. Did the Clerk of the Chambers assign him only minor criminal cases because he was drinking too much, or was he drinking too much because the Clerk assigned him only minor criminal cases? This was very much discussed, every evening, in Penelope and Desmond's new home. It was not the homecoming either of them wanted. Valpy was born in 1947, Tina in 1950, and a week later her favorite uncle, Wilfred Knox, devout Anglo-Catholic who had taken a vow of poverty and presided at her mother's funeral, died, leaving everything he had, which wasn't much, to the Franciscans. When the opportunity to edit *World Review* came along, Penelope and Desmond jumped at it. Penelope was not sure what Desmond thought, but she hoped it would reset everything, the intellectual work rekindling the way they used to be together.

"Cheers," Penelope said, lifting the glass of champagne they couldn't afford and shouldn't have bought.

Desmond smiled gallantly and tipped his glass in her direction.

Tina, who was two and a half, was oblivious, but Valpy knew they were supposed to be celebrating and made them touch glasses properly.

"With a clink," he insisted. And so they clinked.

Just then a wave of nausea threatened to overwhelm her, and she put her hand to her mouth. She turned to Desmond, already pouring a second glass, but he noticed nothing. The next day she went to see the doctor to confirm what she feared.

"Now you have to go," the bank manager said. "Three children under six? How will you manage?"

She had no idea. Life was hard enough with two babies, endless worry about fevers and colds and arranging for sitters so she could get any work done.

She put the Mexico plans in motion.

By the time she took Tina to her mother-in-law's house in Chelsea, she was three months pregnant. Tina, usually stoic, began to cry.

"She will adjust," Penelope said. "She's very brave."

"She's flushed. Does she have a fever?"

"Of course not," Penelope said.

But she did, so Penelope rang Desmond and said she would be staying the night to help settle Tina. "This means you will have to watch Valpy."

"Where is he?" Desmond asked.

"In all likelihood playing with George Wilson next door."

"That's fine. Will he come home on his own?"

"Not typically. Mathilda will give them tea and ring before sending him home. All right?" She waited.

"Yes."

"Mathilda Wilson won't send him home if you're not there."

"All right, yes," Desmond said. "I'll be there."

This meant he would not be at the Duke of Hamilton or the Wells Tavern, off Well Walk. He would not be farther afield at the Old Bull and Bush, from where he'd once come home with Laurence Olivier's autograph. It meant he would not be found, for that night at least, on his regular stool in one of three Red Lions, two White Harts, or the Elephant and Castle. Of course, it did mean he could entertain their friends at Chestnut Lodge, but she had a hard time imagining him doing this without her help.

They figured out that airmail would take a minimum of five

days to reach her. If he wrote every day by morning post, the letters would arrive daily and she could reply in the same manner, and in this way they would keep the business of *World Review* going.

"It will require patience and careful planning," Desmond said. She did not say what she was thinking, but apparently her expression gave her away.

"Which you are always doing anyway," Desmond agreed. "Fine. Perhaps I'll surprise you."

The November issue, with a new story from one of her favorite writers, Alberto Moravia, was due back from the printer any day. Desmond said if it didn't arrive before she left, he would send on a copy. "Don't," she said. "That's too expensive." He looked glum, but didn't argue.

At her mother-in-law's that night, Penelope's dream changed. Now she had to smooth dozens of banknotes with her palms, then hand them over to the sour-looking bank manager, her uncles Dillwyn and Wilfred and the still-alive Ronnie looking on. The Knox family had never had a lot of money, but always just enough, and her father (a poet and editor of *Punch*) and his three brothers (the mathematician at Bletchley, the saint, and a theologian at Oxford) were extraordinary in their fields. She'd always assumed she would be able to raise her family the same way.

Tina woke in the morning fever-free, and two days later, arriving at Euston Station with a small overseas trunk and Valpy, Penelope had an idea that made a sudden, calamitous sense to her. She would not bring Valpy. Of course not! It was too much on him, a little boy being made to earn a legacy. She would deposit him with the stationmaster, and Desmond would retrieve him after work. Tina could stay where she was. Penelope would go to the Delaneys and make their case and be back by the end of the month.

But how could she not bring him? He was a delightful child; kind and observant, quiet. The Delaney sisters would be charmed by how he'd learned to read early and how well he drew. He was drawing now, beside her on the bench, working with a pencil nub. She'd bought him new clothes for the trip, but not pencils. She wanted him to look his best. Wasn't that fair?

She was, however, starting to worry it was the beginning of greed, if greed had a beginning and was not just the way one was born, as she had always suspected.

Desmond had tried one time, in the middle of the night, to talk her out of the plan. All she had to do was ask how much he'd spent at the pub that night and he was quiet.

"I could go with you," he said.

She didn't answer. They both knew that wouldn't work.

In the station Penelope drifted off and dreamed of banknotes. When she opened her eyes, Valpy had finished his picture of Squires Mount, the smaller house they'd recently left for Chestnut Lodge.

"We missed the train, Mama," he said. "But don't worry. There's another in twenty-five minutes."

·· *Day of the Dead* ··

Valpy opened the once-blue door and stared at their trunk in the hallway.

"It's not a miracle," Penelope said.

"But we didn't see or hear him."

"Because we fell asleep. I'm certain Jesús will turn out to be a butler."

Penelope dragged the trunk into the room and unlocked it. Valpy began putting his clothes in the lowest drawer of the wardrobe.

"Thank you, Valpy. I don't bend as easily at the moment."

"I know. And it will only get worse."

She put a protective hand to her as yet small belly, but didn't disagree.

They unpacked in silence. It didn't take very long. All their clothes fit easily in the wardrobe. They hung their coats on the back of the door and arranged a few toiletries on the shelf over the basin. Valpy placed his neatly folded nightshirt on his pillow. Penelope put the bottle of scent Desmond had given her on the windowsill. He'd liked the name, L'Heure Bleue, meant to suggest the moment of dusk just before the stars came out. "I thought you might like something elegant for the mission," he'd said. Seeing her face, he tried again. "I thought it might inspire you. I'm sorry if it's not the right sort of thing." It really wasn't. Another dress would have been far more useful. She had only three: a dark blue, a dark green, and a Liberty print for special occasions, should there be any. Her friend Beryl had tried to give her a polka-dotted one, but that was ridiculous and she'd told her so.

Desmond was truly sorry and she forgave him. How could she not? It was a miracle the elaborate glass bottle, with its inverted heart stopper, hadn't broken in transit.

She looked around the room. It was a pleasure to arrange their few things in a small space, not at all like Chestnut Lodge, where there were still unpacked boxes in every room. She was not a particularly good housekeeper, but found it easy to stay organized when traveling. She placed her notebook—red for this trip, a bit of a joke to herself about their bank account—on the chairless desk by the window.

"Mama, look. There are painters on the roof." On the flat rooftop of the building next to them, two people had set up easels. The man seemed agitated, but the woman was laughing. She was sitting on a folding chair, wearing a printed skirt and white blouse with a circle of large red beads at her neck. As Penelope and Valpy watched, the two swapped work materials. The man shoved the watercolor box with his foot toward the woman. She handed him the palette, then scooted her chair farther away. As they resettled, the man saw Penelope and Valpy in the window. He stared a moment, then mimicked Valpy's posture. Embarrassed, Penelope was going to pull Valpy away, but just then the woman turned to wave, and Valpy waved back.

"Can I paint on the roof?" he said.

"No. We should go down. It's time."

"Do we have to?"

"Yes."

He didn't argue. He rarely did.

"BIENVENIDOS A LA SALA," Chela said grandly, a fresh marigold behind her ear. Somehow she had predicted their descent, appearing precisely as they reached the last stair.

From the marigold-decorated front hall they passed through a small antechamber where there was a short, slight man a little older than Penelope. He wore a blue suit, not particularly well cut, but stood with a very erect posture. Chela acknowledged him, "Mr. Azuela," then made a sound in her throat, impossible to determine if it was sympathetic or the opposite. "What is the state of the mine?" she asked.

"Excellent," he replied, staring straight ahead. He seemed calm, but tired. "What is the state of the house?"

"Excellent. Always," Chela said.

The drawing room was large, yet somehow smaller than Penelope had expected given the size of the house. The shutters were closed across the windows, leaving the room lit only by narrow lines of sun through the slightly turned slats. There was a fragrance of furniture polish, dust, and more marigolds. Armchairs, sofas, settees, all beautiful but far past their prime, were askew, haphazardly arranged on the tiled floor, so that no seating area was particularly well defined. The result of a party or a hastily concluded meeting? Hard to know. The oil paintings and gilt mirrors on the walls were crooked and a Bechstein piano in the corner listed slightly to the right, so earthquake didn't seem entirely far-fetched to Penelope. Several birdcages hung from the ceiling, though they appeared to be empty, and a few tall, broad-leafed plants by the windows looked thirsty. A dozen potted marigolds decorated a tiered table with plates of food and sweets, including a sugar calavera with the name William on the forehead. A Victrola in the corner was playing opera.

Of considerable concern: there were no books. Penelope had always lived in homes with books in every room, hallway, even the pantry, although the pantry at Squires Mount had been, regrettably, quite damp, and a number of volumes were lost. To Penelope a drawing room without books was like a garden without plants.

At the far end of the room, in a pair of red wingback chairs on either side of the fireplace, two women in black dresses and hats with short veils sat quietly. The mantel behind them was laden with silver—candlesticks, bowls, platters, and picture frames—all highly polished. The silver seemed to bring more light into the room.

Chela cleared a path toward the women. "Doña Elena?" She addressed the woman on the right, whose veil was very straight.

"Doña Anita?" Now the one on the left, who had pushed hers up to reveal the tip of her nose. "The two we expected yesterday are here."

"Now? But we just got back from the cemetery," Doña Elena said.

"Jesús did a beautiful job with the flowers," said Doña Anita.

Valpy looked up, but Penelope shook her head.

Chela turned to make sure Penelope and Valpy had followed her through the furniture. "I've put them in the blue room."

Doña Elena reached for some papers on a small table beside her. Penelope was fairly certain she recognized her own stationery.

"I'll leave you," Chela said and threaded her way out.

Penelope wasn't sure whether to sit or stand. She aimed for a small settee upholstered in black-and-white ticking, angling it slightly toward the women in the wingback chairs as she sat with Valpy.

"Single or a widow?" began Doña Elena. Her voice was strong, imposing, but Doña Anita was distracted by a tiny feather lodged in the lace of her veil.

Penelope looked back and forth between them. "What? I am married. I thought you knew."

Doña Elena consulted the letters again, moving one to the top and raising it into a ray of dusty light to see it better. "Oh, yes, Mrs. Fitzgerald. Full name?"

"Penelope Mary Fitzgerald, née Knox."

"Have you any other children dependent on you?"

"Yes, a daughter."

"Called?"

"Christina Rose. Called Tina."

"And where is she?"

"She's two years old. She's with her grandmother in Chelsea."

Doña Elena made a strange, not entirely pleasant face. "How nice you have family you can rely on. Is your mother well?"

"She's my mother-in-law. But yes, to the best of my knowledge."

"Ah. To the best of my knowledge, my sister-in-law is also well. And yet."

Now Doña Anita smiled. "Yes, it is headaches. Stomachaches too. There's a pain in my back, though sometimes I feel it more in my shoulder. And today I find I cannot rotate my right ankle counterclockwise." She stuck out her leg to demonstrate.

Valpy lifted one of his to test himself, but Penelope stopped him with a hand to his knee.

Doña Elena was still looking at Anita, smiling, but not kindly. "And my brother had such a strong constitution." She shook her head. "Do you require extra pillows?" Doña Elena asked, returning to her papers.

"One has always been sufficient," Penelope says.

"Do you rise early or go to bed late?"

Historically, all questions of bedtime had concerned him, so Valpy answered. "I don't mind bedtime, Mrs. Delaney. I never have. I can read if I wake up early."

"You may call me Doña Elena or Señora Delaney or simply Doña. How old are you?"

"Almost seven." He paused, considering his options. "Doña."

"Thank you for inviting us," Penelope said, feeling it imperative to get a word in and begin clarifying things. "Your letter came just when . . ."

But the birdcage over Doña Elena began to swing. A small green parrot roused itself from the floor, flapped to the perch, and started calling in a desperate pitch. "Jaas-per. Jaaaaas-per."

"Let's see," Doña Elena said, ignoring the heart-wrenching call above her head. "Oh yes. From the blue room, you will admire the mountains, everyone does, but don't be fooled. They are farther than they seem."

The bird quieted, its little eyelids closing over shiny black eyes.

"You will need a car if you plan an outing. I hope you brought warm clothing. Fonseca can be chilly at night this time of year. If you need something, Chela will help you."

"What is the bird's name, Doña?" Valpy asked.

"That is Jasper."

"He calls for himself?" Penelope asked.

"No, he was trained to call for a cat of that name who was lost many years ago," Doña Elena said.

"Did he find it?" Valpy asked.

Doña Anita shook her head sadly, and Doña Elena continued. "Avoid the northeast corner of the house. My brother died there, and it is the coldest part of Mirando."

Doña Anita roused herself. "He would have wanted them to have something after their long journey." She gestured at the table covered in marigolds. "Help yourself. My husband has already eaten."

There was a crash from the kitchen and some fast words in Spanish. Valpy pointed at the sugar mask, but Doña Elena frowned.

"That is only for his loved ones to eat. You can take anything else. Is there anything you would like to add to the ofrenda? It is not typical, but if in sixty-six years we are not allowed to bend a few customs to our own needs, then I don't know what we are doing here."

"Oh," Penelope said, "thank you, but we've been traveling."

"You do not travel with mementos of your loved ones?" Doña Elena said.

"I never have."

"Not even a candle?" asks Doña Anita. "Do you have many loved ones?"

"There were three uncles," Penelope said defensively. "Only one is left though."

"Ah, the cart!" cried Doña Anita.

Through a passage connecting the kitchen to the drawing room, Chela wheeled in a little mobile bar. A pitcher of amber liquid stood next to a bowl of ice and another of beheaded marigolds.

"Whiskey marigolds for Día de los Muertos. My own recipe. Whiskey, sherry, orange bitters, and marigold blossom. You must float the flower on top." She looked at Valpy. "There is a bottle of agua fresca for you." Then she turned back to the Doñas. "Shall I let them in? It is already half past five."

Doña Elena held up a hand. It was the chorus of the Hebrew slaves in *Nabucco* playing softly on the Victrola, and she would have no one interrupt it. The room waited, and when it was finished and the needle bumped at the end of the record, she lowered her hand to her chest.

Chela left the drawing room then, passing Mr. Azuela on his way in. Penelope heard the front door open and voices in the hall. More people entered the room. All glanced at Penelope and Valpy, but moved directly toward the Doñas to greet them, some with handshakes, others with hugs. A man in a Bedford cord jacket sat down at the leaning Bechstein and began to play, a stormy étude of the Romantic period. It was loud for conversation, and the piano needed tuning, but Doña Elena smiled.

"Thank you, Mr. Tuttle," she said.

Soon the room was full, the atmosphere more like a small gallery reception than an at home. Groups chatted here and there; everyone helped themselves to Chela's cart. No one spoke to Penelope and Valpy.

"There are no other children," Valpy said.

"Or food," said Penelope. She had no idea what to do, but Chela came to the rescue. She'd prepared dinner for Valpy in the kitchen, she told them. Penelope should go change for the evening. She would send Valpy up when he'd finished.

Having nothing particular to change into, Penelope was still sitting on the chaise in their room when Valpy returned, warm and full.

"What did you have to eat?" Penelope asked.

"It was called queso fundido, the dinner of revolutionaries."

Penelope had some questions, but Valpy continued. "Chela said it is okay that we had nothing for the ofrenda because the whole month of November is devoted to the holy souls in purgatory. There is no way of knowing for sure if your loved ones are in heaven, hell, or purgatory, but we are allowed to pray for them anyway."

"Valpy, the specificity of Catholicism is too much for me at the moment."

He studied her, worried. "She said we can also dance in honor of our loved ones."

Penelope tried to imagine herself dancing for her mother. Christina had been gone half her life, and she'd had no ofrendas to help her remember. Her father could not speak of her, had not even said her name since the day she died when Penelope was eighteen, the summer before she went up to Somerville, her mother's college. Penelope knew her mother was sick but thought she would recover. When she died suddenly on May 30 of peritonitis, a cloud came over Penelope's life that had never left. She gathered up all her mother's books and took them with her to Somerville. If their adult lives could not touch, at least their marginal notes were forever overlaid and intertwined.

"What if we aren't dancers," she said.

"I asked the same thing! 'Impossible,' Chela said. 'Everyone dances.'"

Valpy climbed into bed. "Where is the northeast corner of the house?"

"I don't know, but don't worry. If you need an extra jumper, we will get you one."

DOWNSTAIRS THE DRAWING ROOM was still full. Chela didn't mention that Penelope hadn't changed, but it was obvious from her expression she didn't approve. Penelope thanked her for feeding Valpy.

"He ate well," Chela said. It sounded like a rebuke, and Penelope was not sure how to defend herself. Eating on the bus journey had been complicated. She asked for a glass of water. Chela handed her an agua fresca. "Should I explain everything now?" she said.

"Please," said Penelope.

The evening drink at Mirando was generally sherry, with special cocktails on Wednesdays and Saturdays. Today was an exception because of the holiday, Chela said, though Penelope would soon learn there were many exceptions because of the many Catholic holidays. On Fridays the Doñas refrained, and on Sundays they celebrated the Lord's day with champagne. Drinks were at five, dinner was at seven, and it was only for the guests at Mirando: Mr. and Mrs. Tuttle, Mr. Flatley, occasionally Mr. Azuela, the Doñas, and now, of course, Penelope and Valpy.

"Flatley?" Penelope said.

"An Irish tutor. He may suggest lessons for your son, but you should refuse. Thursdays the Doñas take a cold plate and the others eat out. That is my evening off." She poured a whiskey marigold and handed it to Penelope, but Penelope thought she better clarify a few things before she took a sip.

"There are people who are staying at Mirando, and others who come to Mirando only in the evening?"

"Sí." Chela looked around the room. "Mrs. Slater comes often." She indicated a smartly dressed woman with well-cut auburn hair. "She's American, and her husband is an engineer. She wants to make an arts center somewhere. There is Señor Molina. He has many ideas, some good. Mrs. Clancy comes when she is not busy in the mountain villages." Chela looked annoyed at the thought. "I don't see Señor Garza tonight, but he wants to establish the first national bird museum. Others come and go. It is very time-consuming and expensive. But anyone who wishes to have business with the Doñas calls at this time."

"Every day?" Penelope asked.

"Every day."

"But what kind of business?"

Chela clicked her tongue. "Mrs. Fitzgerald. I believe you already know." She dropped a marigold in Penelope's drink and went back to the kitchen.

Agua fresca in one hand, whiskey marigold in the other, Penelope headed toward a red settee that might have once been paired with the chaise in her room. It was large enough for two, but by placing herself squarely in the middle, she hoped to avoid company. She needn't have worried; no one approached her, though she did notice Mrs. Slater and Mrs. Clancy eyeing her, first separately and then in intimate conversation with each other. Both were dressed in neat blouses with matching cardigans. Mrs. Slater looked about Penelope's age, Mrs. Clancy was older. All the visitors, callers, drop-ins—Penelope didn't know how to think of them—mingled and chatted in small groups, occasionally breaking off to refill their drinks at the cart, admire the ofrenda, or converse privately with the Doñas. Penelope heard whispers of plans for hospital wings, garden clubs, and silver guilds. After a time, Chela lit a fire and several people offered toasts, in English, to the Doñas' generosity and hospitality. Señor Molina addressed the room about a plan for a fleet of bookmobiles to be dispatched throughout the state of Coahuila, but when he was finished Doña Elena said there was already the great State Public Library on the Alameda Zaragoza. Molina argued that not everyone had transportation to the great library. His plan was inspired by the Red Cross traveling librarians during the war. Their work had been invaluable, he said, in revealing what people really wanted to read when they genuinely needed an imaginative escape.

"And what do they want?" Doña Elena asked.

Penelope's ears pricked. She wanted to know, but Molina sputtered and the Doñas' attention moved on.

The light was fading over the square, the bright lines between the shutter slats growing dimmer. Every time Penelope thought about not having to organize dinner or unpack Chestnut Lodge, she was relieved. But every time she thought the legacy must be an open secret and everyone in Fonseca had a plan for it, she took a sip of the whiskey marigold.

Before bed, Penelope began a list. She thought she had better begin keeping track of the competition:

- *Mr. Azuela: longtime manager of the silver mine formerly owned by the Delaneys, now nationalized. Still reporting to the Doñas?*
- *Mr. and Mrs. Tuttle: penniless organist and his wife. Childless?*
- *Mr. Flatley: Irish tutor, clever but difficult to like. Students?*

- *Señor Molina: bookmobiles.*
- *Señor Garza: bird museum.*
- *Father Bedoya: Catholic priest, the usual parish needs.*
- *Mrs. Slater: arts center.*

She listed others by the proposals she'd overheard:

- *Hospital Wing*
- *Garden Club and Azalea Society*
- *Silver Guild*

That night Penelope dreamed of her mother, waking at half past two with a sob, highly unusual for her, both the waking and the sobbing. She blamed the whiskey marigold.

PENELOPE MET VIOLET SLATER the next day. She came upon her staring at Mirando's polished staircase.

"Irish oak," Violet whispered, large hazel eyes wide. "Can you imagine?"

Penelope studied the banister, not sure what she was supposed to be imagining.

Within a few days, Penelope understood Violet Slater was interested in Mirando itself, as Mirando stood just outside the main shopping district of the Zona Centro and in this way was perfect for the arts center she wanted. She'd studied English at Smith and dreamed of staging *Romeo and Juliet*, using the little rounded balcony on Mirando's second floor for act 2, scene 2. Her son, Milo, a bit older than Valpy, was a born thespian, she said.

Violet's friend, Rose Clancy, was an Irish expat like the Doñas, married to an insurance executive, childless. The Clancys kept the only key to the only fire truck in Fonseca, employed a cook who was a cousin of the chief of police, and hosted an annual chicken fry for the entire European and American expat community in Fonseca. She wanted a community outreach center that would run tours and day trips to small Mexican villages for aid and instruction.

"Clancy means red warrior," she told Penelope when they met. She said it with a jaunty smile, but the meaning was clear.

Two flowers, Violet and Rose. Together they planned to shape Fonseca into something they liked better. Violet Slater, especially, was the kind of woman Penelope feared. Refined, calm, put together, she could say something untoward and get away with it. And the only thing Penelope liked about Mrs. Clancy was her gray hair.

Penelope's list now also included Mr. Whishaw, the Doñas' bank manager with the Banco de Londres y México, not because he was competing for the legacy, but because he seemed to be the only one who possessed any definite information about it. His cousin, also a Mr. Whishaw, a solicitor with the same firm, came to Mirando too.

Penelope also noted the house staff: the formidable Chela, who was not live-in, but sometimes slept in the room over the kitchen if she had a lot of cooking to do or a feast-day meal to prepare. Her beautiful young cousin, Esperanza, with delicate features and long eyelashes, came on Tuesdays to help with laundry and cleaning, but never seemed to get very much done. Another quarter cousin came on saints' days to do the same. And finally Jesús, solemn but irritable, who wore only white shirts and black trousers and whose glasses were continually smudged. He was driver, gardener, and handyman all in one.

What had she been expecting? A series of teas with two sweet, elderly Doñas and Valpy in a cozy house? Actually, yes. Something like that. Certainly not a strange house full of guests, and a town full of people, all of them hoping for the legacy too.

She had packed half a dozen issues of *World Review* to share with the Doñas, including their most recent with a short story by Dylan Thomas. She had a business plan, a dream table of contents (she was hoping to get something from Beckett), a ledger of production, printing, and distribution costs. She'd even brought paper stock samples. She stacked everything in a pile beneath the chaise.

At the bottom of her list, Penelope added herself:

- P. Fitzgerald, coeditor of an English literary journal, writer. Friend of the family?

In a letter to Desmond she labeled them all, herself included, Pretenders. "The situation is more complex than I could have imagined," she wrote.

When he responded, he reminded her that the term "pretender" was not in itself pejorative. The original meaning of the English word "pretend," from the French *prétendre*, simply meant "to put forward, to profess or claim."

"Don't give up. I'd put you up against a Mrs. Slater any day," he wrote. "And what could the priest possibly have on you? I'd only worry about that ornithologist. A bird museum sounds like a good idea."

## ·· *Resolve* ··

"Valpy, the Doñas are not what I expected. Mirando is not what I expected. Truly, nothing is as I expected."

It was the end of their first week and Valpy was drawing. Without a chair, he had taken to sitting on top of the desk by the window, cross-legged, elbows on his knees over his paper.

"But it doesn't matter," Penelope said. "We are going to stay. One way or another we will have an interesting time."

"A big time?"

"What?"

Valpy reminded her that they'd heard a woman on the bus in Knoxville use this expression. Neither had been sure what it meant.

"I think so." Later, Penelope would marvel at her determination. She would remember the first days after arriving in Fonseca as sun filled and tantalizingly warm, but confusing. The competition for the legacy registered as a pit in her stomach, but they had to stay. Chestnut Lodge, *World Review*, the kind of upbringing she wanted for her children—all depended on her success. If there was to be a contest, she had entered it.

"How long will we stay?" Valpy asked.

"I don't know yet."

"Until February twenty-second?"

"I shouldn't think that long. Why?"

"It is a sad anniversary. The streets run with tears."

"Did Chela say that?"

Valpy nodded. He'd had breakfast with Chela in the kitchen three times, and already he was sounding like her. "Come at eight, not one minute before," she'd told him. "That is the hour all the ovens are opened and you can smell the fresh bread."

Valpy was skeptical. "All the ovens can't be opened at the same time."

"Then where does the smell come from? Doña Lopez can smell it as far as the Santo Cristo del Ojo de Agua, which she attends with her son and daughter-in-law."

"I don't know where that is," Valpy said.

"The carts arrive just before the hour. You'll feel the town tremble from their wheels. You don't believe me? Your windows will rattle in their frames!"

"I won't be scared."

"Good. After that you may come to the kitchen. What do you like to eat?"

"Eggs and toast."

"You'll have chilaquiles and machaca."

Valpy had no idea what those were. "Thank you," he said.

Penelope believed in routine, though was not always good at

making one. In Fonseca, however, she prevailed. Monday through Friday Valpy had lessons in the morning with the sisters of San Esteban. She had declined Mr. Flatley's offer. In the afternoons he helped Jesús in the garden, Chela in the kitchen, or went with Penelope on an outing or errand. He ate supper early in the kitchen with Chela and was upstairs for the evening by six o'clock. Saturday was for sight-seeing, and Sunday everyone attended Mass with the Doñas. Penelope had not brought a hat, but Chela loaned her a scarf so she could cover her head.

"I know why the house is called Mirando," Valpy told Penelope one morning. They were exploring the garden. From the street, you would never imagine the house to be hiding such a large expanse of nature. There were really two gardens linked by a trellis and a few steps: first a rose garden with box hedges and a small brick terrace, then through the arch a small lawn with borders full of jasmine, camellias, dahlias, gardenias, and other perennials, everything labeled with copper plant markers. They were walking along slowly, reading.

"Why?"

"It means watching."

"Watching what?" Penelope asked.

"Everything, Chela says. Two cultures watching each other, trying to figure out an advantage."

"Who named it that?"

"I don't know."

"Valpy, Chela tells you a lot of stories."

"I tell her stories too. I told her about the bathrooms for Mexicans in America."

"Oh dear. What did she say?"

"She says we better not go back that way."

Valpy took out his drawing pad. "She told me about Jasper."

"The parrot or the cat?"

"Both. Jasper wasn't trained to call for him. The bird learned from the boy Doña Elena hired to call Jasper's name. Hour after hour he walked the streets of the Zona Centro so that everyone from Mirando to the Plaza de Armas had a terrible headache until he was found."

"But I thought he wasn't found," Penelope said.

"That's what the Doñas think. Chela found him half-eaten by a coyote and dropped at the kitchen door. Can we buy some paint?"

"That's a very good idea. And maybe we can take a few days away from Mirando. Maybe we should go to the mountains."

"How? They are farther than they seem."

Back in their room, Valpy wanted to make lists. He tore a piece of paper in two and gave half to Penelope. She smoothed it with her palm. What did she want? She could think of so many things. Time, attention, a trip to St. Petersburg, a well-tailored coat, a soft jumper in a color she doesn't even know suits her, a bouquet of fresh flowers, a book she's never heard of, a poem, a drawing, a sense of direction, her mother. This practice of listing what you *want* but don't really *need* came from her grandfather Edmund Knox, who rose from a poor vicarage family to become bishop of Manchester, living proof of the power of the exercise. She wrote:

- *a parrot*
- *a rainy day*
- *a serape*

They made lists when they were anxious or unsatisfied, and Penelope usually made sure to include something within Valpy's range. Possibly a mistake, as it could lead to a lifetime of believing he could make other people happy. He read her list. "I thought you would include a hat."

"I'm lacking a hat, it's true, but I don't really want one. I want a parrot, but I don't need one."

Valpy began drawing a bird. "Parrots can live a hundred years," he said. "Mama, did Don Guillermo die because it is the coldest part of the house, or is it the coldest part of the house because he died there?"

"Who is Don Guillermo?"

"Doña Anita's husband! Mama, are you paying attention?" He showed her his list, now with a little bird for her in the corner.

- *a cat*
- *a ride on an airplane*
- *a very warm jumper*

"That is a good bird," Penelope said, and she began to draw a jumper. She liked to draw everyday objects with an old-fashioned sense of space and line. It was something of a family practice; her father and Desmond did the same. "Don't worry about the jumper. The one you have is warm enough."

"Can we burn them now?" This was the last part of the ritual.

"I don't have any matches."

"You should put them on your list."

THE FOLLOWING SATURDAY there were whiskey sours and to everyone's surprise it was raining, daring even to gust at times. This kept many of the day visitors away, and drinks that evening included only the houseguests and Mr. Azuela, who arrived wearing his usual blue suit, but very wet.

"Did you walk?" Doña Elena said, her tone withering. "If your driver is off, you should take the bus. I took the bus—"

"Where!" Doña Anita cried.

"Not recently! But I remember taking the bus once. A passenger boarded with a large bill the driver couldn't change. The driver waved him on, saying he'd change it when he could, and when the time came the passengers passed the bill forward, hand to hand, all the way from the back of the bus to the front. The correct change was then returned in the same manner, hand to hand, all the way from the front to the back. Isn't that extraordinary?"

Doña Anita was frowning. "What is extraordinary?"

"These were very poor people, Anita."

"So you are impressed they didn't steal it?"

Doña Elena set her face for confrontation. "A thirsty man will raise his tongue for even a drop of rain."

"Maybe in the movies," Mr. Tuttle said.

"Oh, you are thinking of *The Grapes of Wrath*," said Mr. Flatley.

Mr. Azuela, who had been hoping to get a word in, raised his hand. "I would like to say that I have never had a driver."

"How would one of them have made off with the money though?" Penelope was sorry to be the one thinking like a criminal, but it couldn't be helped. "Was the bus in motion?"

"That is not the point," said Doña Elena.

"No," said Doña Anita. "That is the point." She put her hand to her forehead. "Wait, what was the point?"

Doña Elena smiled unkindly. "Is your ankle working now? Shoulder feeling better? Another whiskey?"

"I am your brother's widow!" Anita snapped. "You should be nicer to me."

Doña Elena turned to Mr. Azuela. "Tell us about the mine. How is it going? Is the government treating you well?"

"Oh, thank you, Doña. It is fine. The shaft at Arteaga is still yielding, and we're breaking ground soon on two open-pits."

"Mrs. Slater tells me her husband has a plan for more underground operations," Doña Elena said.

Mr. Azuela's face changed. "The Slater plan for cheaper ventilation and communication is reckless and irresponsible," he said.

"She says the displaced soil and rock from open-pit operations damages flora and fauna."

Mr. Azuela hesitated.

"A pity she is not here this evening to persuade you," Elena said.

"If you are worried about local fauna, Doña," Mr. Azuela began, "we could discuss the donkeys. Since we stopped using the arrastra—"

"Oh the arrastra made more dust in an already arid climate," Elena said dismissively. "I am for the new extraction methods."

"Yes, but what are we to do about the donkeys? What are these poor animals to do now that they are no longer needed to pull the arrastras? Have you seen a decommissioned donkey?"

"How would I recognize it?"

"Generalized dullness, shifting weight, motionless ears."

"That describes all the donkeys I have ever seen."

"Then you have never seen a healthy donkey!" cried Mr. Azuela.

"Silver has no rhyme in English," Doña Anita said. She was brooding now, sullen. "It's not the most precious metal, but it is the most reflective and malleable. I've always liked it."

Doña Elena ignored her, and Chela announced dinner, her normally smooth and coiled braid loose down her back, a few frizzy strands framing her face. She was rushed and irritated. "Did someone wish for rain?" she demanded.

Dear ——

Apologies for the delay in replying, I have been traveling. Here are a few reminiscences of the trip to Mexico to the Purcell (not "Delaney") family in Saltillo (not "Fonseca") which I trust will interest you. I have tried to respond to your queries as best I can. Quite a Proustian exercise for me as you can imagine.

We took the RMS *Queen Mary* from Liverpool to New York, very luxurious. My main memories are of the waves in the swimming pool, the enormous reception rooms, and sitting in deckchairs swaddled in blankets with bowls of bouillon. Apparently, Bing Crosby was on the ship and gave me his autograph.

The trip must have been expensive and it is not clear how it was financed because PM & D were not well off. Most likely funded, at least in part, by Desmond's parents.

I have vivid memories of playing in the gardens of the house with the gardener Jesús. I was amazed that anyone could be called "Jesús" at all. I helped him weed the vegetable patch, although he was annoyed when I pulled up the carrots to look at them.

We went to mass on Sundays in the cathedral with the sisters in their veils. PM was an observant Anglican, but took her marriage commitment to bringing me up as a Catholic very seriously.

Just why PM referred to Saltillo as "Fonseca" in her article on plotting is a mystery. There is no town of "Fonseca" in Mexico, but recently we discovered an old family atlas with a cross marked on Saltillo in what appears to be Desmond's penmanship.

Best wishes,<br>Valpy

## ·· The Market ··

Fonseca had two markets, and the little donkey tied up for rides between them was soft gray, with a white-tipped muzzle and a touch of white under each eye. It stood next to a group of mariachis, its legs braced at a wide angle, its neck low, ears limp, all surprisingly still for a live animal. It was wearing a red serape and silver bells on its harness, but these only sounded when a child was dropped on its back. Then the spindly legs shook, the back sank farther, and the donkey strained and staggered, its gray lips flaring over huge yellow teeth while the mariachis played. The total effect was of a creature pushed beyond any reasonable limit, openly in need of rescue.

"Behold," said Mr. Azuela. "A decommissioned donkey." He seemed pale and sweaty, as if he hadn't showered for a few days or had suffered night sweats.

The outing was Doña Elena's idea. The evening before, she'd ordered Mr. Azuela to give them a tour of the town. He clearly had business at the mine, and Penelope and Valpy had been sightseeing a bit on their own, but she would not be deterred. "You should see something a local can show you," she insisted after a number of French 75s. Her eyes flashed. "Take them to the mercado, Mr. Azuela," she said. "Take them all the way in."

"He would have once proudly pulled the arrastra," Mr. Azuela said now, "grinding silver ore with a team of his fellows. Unfortunately for burros, pain makes dullness."

Penelope, firmly believing this was true for people, too, tried to steer Valpy away, but she was too late. As they watched, a father, a tourist judging from his clothes, paid for his son to have a ride. The mariachi began, and the man hoisted his boy onto the beast's back. The impact made the animal bleat and stagger a few steps, then collapse. The father pulled the crying boy out from under the animal. Was he hurt? No, the tears were because he didn't get to finish his ride! The father, humiliated in front of the growing crowd, demanded his money back, but one of the mariachis insisted they try again and dragged the donkey up by the halter. This time, after a quick drink of water, the animal held. The music began again, and the father got his picture.

"Did you know," Mr. Azuela said, "that a donkey can recognize a place or companion for up to twenty-five years?"

The father lifted his son off the exhausted animal, and they headed into the new market. The mariachis waited. A fly walked up the donkey's nose, then across one eyeball.

"That poor animal," Penelope said. "How can they treat it so terribly?"

"The men are poor, too, Mrs. Fitzgerald."

Valpy began to cry.

"Can we see something else, please?" Penelope said.

Mr. Azuela turned and moved them toward the market on the other side of the street. "Of course. We are heading to the old mercado, anyway. It is more authentic. It was erected, together with the bullring, by a benefactor. A native of the town, a successful banderillero who wanted to give back to the place of his birth."

Mr. Azuela had cast off his reluctance to participate in this outing and seemed to be enjoying himself. His eyebrows were dark and expressive. He gestured grandly to the market across the street. "The supermercado was built by the Providence Clancy Insurance Company after the old mercado burned down."

Penelope stared at the outer circle of the old mercado, where there were sweet stalls displaying years-old mazapán figures and graying chocolate. The rest of it was a forest of rotting planks and struts stuck in the ground here and there in order to hold up slanted pieces of corrugated metal.

"It burned down?" Valpy said.

"Yes! But rose again, such as it is. Not everyone can afford the supermercado, you see."

The next circle had clothes and household goods, all used, mostly broken. You could buy one shoe at a time or half a cigarette. Then came a circle where pieces of fruit and sugarcane, charms, aphrodisiacs, and medicine tablets were all arranged in heaps and sold by the handful. And then Mr. Azuela brought them right into the innermost ring, where the fishmongers and butchers threw the eyes and entrails behind their stalls. Penelope put a hand to her throat, worried she was going to be sick. "Perhaps a souvenir?" Mr. Azuela said.

They followed him out again, stopping at a toy stall on the perimeter filled with rough pottery figures. A tourist stood marveling. "This is the work of an artist, you can see it," the tourist said, holding up a clay pitcher in the shape of a horse.

"Yes, the children are very talented, señora," Mr. Azuela said. "Their fingers are small and they learn early."

The woman's smiled faded. She set the horse pitcher down gently, pretended to look a bit more, then started to drift away.

The shopkeeper grabbed a candlestick. "Señora, mira, look. This is not made by children. It is a sirena, a mermaid. She is lovely." The figure's head and waist rose on one side of the candle opening, her arms wrapped around a lute. Her mermaid tail, looking a bit like two cacti side by side, rose on the reverse. The tourist smiled, but shook her head and left.

The shopkeeper turned on Mr. Azuela, speaking in very fast Spanish.

"Here, let me purchase a gift for you," he said quickly to Penelope and Valpy. "Maybe a cochinito, a piggy bank?" He scanned the crowded table and chose one, a pink pig painted with purple roses, but Valpy shook his head. Instead Valpy chose a white lamb whose coat was made to look fluffy with tiny white knobs like braille. It stood on a green platform, its belly over a rise of clay shaped into a little hillock blooming with yellow flowers. Of all the figures on the table, Penelope thought it was the sweetest. There was something about the legs that captured well the precarious balance of a young animal. Only the snout seemed off, a bit long, wolfish, and there were, somewhat inexplicably, two pink circles on both haunches.

A slit along the back was for the coins, but when Penelope turned it over, she saw there was no larger cork or plastic plug in the belly. "It only has one opening," she said, turning the lamb over again. "How do you get the money out?"

"Ah, that is the gracia of the cochinito, señora," the shopkeeper said. "When you have saved you must break everything and begin again."

"But what if you want to keep it as a souvenir?"

"I don't mind, Mama," Valpy said, taking the lamb back again. "I'll give it to Tina. She doesn't have any money anyway."

The shopkeeper, who was already wrapping the lamb in newspaper, stopped. "It is bad luck not to give the cochinito a full belly," she said.

"Then I'll help my sister fill it." Valpy spoke with surprising determination.

The shopkeeper resumed wrapping. "All right. But when the time comes you must help her break it also."

Valpy nodded, but Penelope could see his moment of bravery had passed. She knew he would never break the lamb bank.

The next stall sold sweet calaveras of indeterminate age. Some looked relatively fresh; others might have been years old. The holiday had passed, of course, but the item was popular with tourists, and so they were always available. Some had a space on the forehead to add a name of the buyer's choosing; others already had the name written in sugar. Almost immediately Penelope saw one that said Christina and felt weak in the knees. A moment earlier she would have said this was just an expression, but when she dipped and had to steady herself with a hand to the edge of the table, she knew it was an accurate description of an unwelcome surprise.

Mr. Azuela took his leave of them; he was overdue at the mine. He had to meet Mr. Slater that afternoon at Arteaga, ten miles from Fonseca. He looked at Valpy. "Perhaps you'd like to see the mine one day," he said. "The open-pits are very impressive. The stepped walls look like an inverted Teotihuacan. I bet you'd like that."

Valpy looked to Penelope, who deflected the question by inquiring how long Mr. Azuela had been at the mine.

"It is the only job I have ever had, and my father before me, and his father before him. The Azuelas have managed the Delaney mines since the early 1800s. We have been miners, engineers, accountants. The government does not know how to run a mine. Only how to profit from it. You know how to find your way back?"

Penelope said she did. But after he left, she steered Valpy, who looked tired and defeated by the day, to a place in the shade. She proposed a stop at the Hotel Arizpe on the way home for an ice cream or lemonade. Her rule was one treat a day, and they already had the lamb bank, but Mr. Azuela had paid for that, and anyway, she felt circumstances called for an exception.

"Not home," Valpy said. "You mean Mirando."

"Of course," she agreed, but now they were both defeated by the day.

The restaurant on the ground floor was green and cool, with plants everywhere and large birdcages hanging from the ceiling, some of them made of wire, others made of bamboo, all of them occupied. Penelope was going to have a bowl of ice cream, but when Valpy wanted only an agua fresca, she just ordered one too. He remained solemn and still until Penelope noticed a couple at another table.

"Valpy, look," she said. "Are those the painters?" They were easily recognizable. He had a tall bald head and was always in a brown jacket; she wore white or printed blouses, usually with a red bead necklace at her throat that Penelope admired. They were both in their late sixties.

When the woman next looked up, she noticed Penelope and Valpy. She said something to the man, then shook her head and left him to come to their table. "Hi," she said, her accent American. "You are the boy in the window." She smiled at Penelope.

"You are the painter on the rooftop," Valpy said.

"Well, one of them." She turned back to her table. "The other one is over there, but he's grumpy."

She had intentionally spoken loudly enough for him to hear, and the brown-jacketed shoulders bristled.

"What are you doing in that window all the time?" she asked. She had a thick bob of gray-white hair that she ran her hand through.

"Drawing," Valpy answered.

"Is that right?"

"How do you get up to the roof?"

"Oh, it's easy. We're staying at Guajardo House, and it's right above our room. We've stayed there before. I'm Jo Hopper." She tilted her head. "That's Edward." She smiled again when she saw the name meant something to Penelope. "Are you on holiday?"

Penelope looked at Valpy. "Yes," she said. "We're visiting friends."

"That's nice. We've visited several times but haven't made any friends. Edward prefers to be alone, up on the roof." She laughed. "But we come here most afternoons for something to eat. Maybe we'll see you again." She looked at Valpy. "Next time bring your notebook and show me your drawings."

Valpy nodded, thrilled, and Penelope had to acknowledge that Jo had saved the day.

Later, when he thought she wasn't looking, Penelope watched Valpy push the lamb bank under his bed as far as his arm would reach.

## ·· *Signs* ··

All she had to do was find a way to distinguish herself in a drawing room halfway across the world. It sounded simple, but it wasn't. The irony of having traveled so far to try for a legacy for her life with a husband who drank too much, only to find the money controlled by two women seemingly drinking themselves to death, was not lost on her.

The Doñas' drinking was staggering. Each evening they began with a glass of sherry. If it was not a cocktail night or a feast day, they would have at least three or four more. If it was a cocktail night, after the sherry they enjoyed two or three of these. Penelope had been at Mirando two weeks, and so far in addition to the whiskey marigolds, there had been Palomas and pink gins, gimlets, martinis, and Manhattans. The wine at dinner was excellent, most of it imported from France, and the Doñas always finished a bottle each. Afterward they had port or brandy, sometimes both, and on

Sundays the champagne was served in the Mirando cut glass flutes, sometimes with two ounces of Guinness, brought in from El Dublín, the Irish pub across the square. This was called a black velvet and had been a favorite of Don Guillermo's.

At this rate of consumption, a very real question might be, how much of the legacy was left? Also striking to Penelope was how evocative the scene was of a story they'd just published in their October issue, "The Followers" by Dylan Thomas. She remembered bits and pieces of the paragraph describing the saloon, where the regulars grew "grand and muzzy in the corners" and "grannies in dustbin black cackled and nipped." There was even a "crippled piano."

She would write to Thomas when she got back and tell him.

Doña Anita began the evenings tired, but after the first drink her light-blue eyes came alive and she was full of merriment, briefly. Several drinks later she began to grow vague. Doña Elena stayed sharper and ran the interviews with the Pretenders. She had an astonishingly good memory for everyone's past troubles, her brown eyes and off-center smile flashing periodically. But there was a fine line between remembering and touching a wound, and Penelope could chart Elena's progress by the expressions of her guests. First a smile as they thanked her, then more serious, then suddenly solemn, then a protective blank. Almost all immediately refreshed their drink after talking with her. A small number left, but not many, devastating evidence of what people were willing to endure for the hope of financial security.

More letters from home began to arrive. Her neighbor Mathilda

Wilson wrote to say George missed Valpy and the front gate of Chestnut Lodge was broken. Her mother-in-law wrote to say Tina was doing well. Penelope would have liked to have had much more news of Tina, and she wrote back to say so. In the next letter her mother-in-law said that Desmond was visiting and they were all three enjoying more time together. She included no news of Tina, but someone had given her the page to make a little scrawl in the corner. It must have been Desmond; her mother-in-law was too neat.

Penelope's father wrote to say the new young queen was planning her first live radio broadcast at Christmas. Would Penelope be able to hear it where she was? And when was she due back again? He couldn't remember. Also, he asked her not to forget her stepmother's birthday Christmas Day. Mary Shepard was only seven years older than Penelope, but they shared many interests and were lucky to be fond of each other. Penelope admired her illustrations for P. L. Travers's Mary Poppins series and, years from now, would be very glad when the Disney company was forced to pay her some compensation because it was her idea that the magical nanny always land with her feet in first position. Penelope's father closed with a drawing of an hourglass in the corner of the page, which felt ominous. She wondered if he was feeling well. He was now seventy-one.

Her friend Jean wrote, "What are you doing down there in Mexico? Of course, it is just the sort of thing you would do. Do you mean to disappear, à la the Franklin expedition?" Penelope was tempted to write back that if she didn't succeed, she may become the *woman* who ate her boots, though there was probably less nutrition in her co-op loafers than the explorer's moccasins. She didn't, however, because it seemed grim and she was superstitious.

Desmond's next letter also mentioned the broken gate at Chestnut Lodge. "That's the bad news. The good news is that I've got Stevie to agree that 'New Novels' will review no more than 3 to 5 at a time. The bad news is I have in hand a terrible review of *Invisible Man* by Ralph Ellison, which is enjoying spectacular notices in the US and here. Bellow called it a 'superb book'; Burgess a 'masterpiece.' Here's a choice sentence from Stevie's review: 'The style of this book is chaotic, which is a pity, as the book has something to say which sounds worth saying when one can catch a word in the uproar.' One wishes we had someone else to take this one. What should we do?"

She wrote back there was nothing to do. Stevie Smith was doing "New Novels" at their invitation, and they knew she was eccentric when they asked her. She did suggest, though, that they run it last in the group of reviews.

"The painters are out again," Valpy said from his perch on the desk in their room. He liked to chart the painters' progress and watch the Mirando doves swoop and soar over the rooftops. "They're arguing."

"Not again."

"Do you think there's a way from our roof to theirs?" he asked.

"No, I don't," Penelope said. "And you will not go looking for one."

"We could go together."

"We are not going to bother the painters."

"Then can we find the northeast corner of the house? You said we would and we haven't."

Penelope agreed, but the task proved difficult. Partly this was because the house was kept shuttered, so there was not much daylight to orient themselves. Penelope calculated Mirando faced east because of the way the light slanted across the square each evening. Then it was a question of which floor the Doña meant. The top floor had a number of small bedrooms just like the one Penelope and Valpy were in. The first floor was where the Doñas slept in bedroom suites, and the ground floor had the drawing room, dining room, and kitchen.

"And there could be a basement," Valpy whispered.

Valpy put on his jumper, and they started at the top, standing in the hallway outside their once-blue door. Penelope turned one way, then the other. "Valpy, it's the loo. That is the northeast corner."

They walked down the hall and stood outside it, Valpy visibly disappointed.

On the first floor an unremarkable hallway ended in a shuttered window. There was a wooden chair and table with some faded photographs in silver frames, several of people on the deck of a ship. Penelope contemplated taking the chair for their room.

"No one dies in a hallway," Valpy said.

Penelope almost asked why not, but as the exercise was meant to reassure him, she stopped herself.

The floor had a sitting room in what seemed to be the right location. Valpy walked around trying every seat. "I'm not cold," he said. "Are you?"

"Not in the least."

They were headed to the ground floor when Valpy tried a closed door at the top of the staircase. Both of them were delighted to discover the door opened into a library with floor-to-ceiling bookcases, several sofas, and a fireplace that looked as if it hadn't been used in years. Penelope was relieved. If the Doñas weren't readers now, as far as she could see, maybe they had been. This might bolster their case for the legacy. As soon as she stepped through the door, however, she shuddered. She tried to conceal it from Valpy, but he was watching her, wide-eyed.

"Valpy," she said. "Mirando is an old building with thick walls, poor heating, and very little sunlight. Of course it's cold."

He was unconvinced.

"Heat rises, which would explain why we were warmer on the upper floor and colder here."

He considered this and began to relax. In addition to the built-in shelves on the walls, the library had a number of free-standing bookcases in an open square in the middle of the room. Inside this was a table with six chairs so that the room had the feel of a small municipal library more than a personal study, and one of these chairs was pulled out, as if recently vacated. Just then they heard a creaking. Penelope was uncertain for a moment, but then identified the sound. "It's those old pecan trees. It's windy today. The branches are rubbing against each other in the wind. I've heard it before."

"So where do you think it happened?" he asked.

"I have no idea. Maybe it didn't. Maybe it is just a story."

"Chela says that when the Doñas leave Mirando to attend Mass on Sundays, the birds stop singing from the time they step out the door until the doors of San Esteban close."

"Enough." She led him out of the library. She did not tell him that as they crossed back over the threshold, she felt a chill and shuddered again.

## ·· The Delaney ··

The next night at Mirando there were pink gins and flowering winter mimosa branches in tall earthenware vases all around the drawing room. Such beauty brought inside was magnificent, but Penelope's own flower arranging tended toward the occasional posy, and she felt overwhelmed. Scattered petals on the floor added to the decadent and untamed mood. Pax batted these around until they disappeared under the furniture.

When Penelope entered the drawing room, there was a man she didn't recognize sitting on what she'd begun to think of as her settee. It was early yet, but this man with black eyes and very black hair, dressed in elegant white-linen clothes, already had a group around him. At the other end of the room, the Doñas were listening to an animated Mr. Azuela, just finishing his report. Penelope, unsure where to go, hesitated too long.

"Ah, Mrs. Fitzgerald," Mrs. Clancy said, catching Penelope's arm, "you might be interested in this." She caught another woman, a member of the Garden Club and Azalea Society, with her other hand. "I was just saying that at the Center for Community Outreach, we explain that the responsibility for contact rests entirely with us, as we're guests in this country. We have six months theory and workshop practice before we go out to the mountain villages. And success is by no means guaranteed."

Garden Club nodded.

Penelope said, "I'm sorry. I thought the center didn't exist yet?"

"I've been lucky enough to get a small group started. But we try not to go too fast, like the time one of our volunteers tried to get the women to slap their tortillas twice with each hand instead of three times," said Mrs. Clancy.

"With what result?" asked the stranger in white, who had approached.

Mrs. Clancy was delighted to have captured his interest. "Well, we learned the three-time rhythm has a soothing effect for them." She put down her drink and began to demonstrate with an imaginary tortilla.

Garden Club watched carefully. Hospital Wing, also nearby, nodded.

"You have to study their mentality, you see, to learn where it is worth pressing a point," Mrs. Clancy continued. "Of course, you have to be careful not to go the other way and feel that there's nothing to be done to beat their cradle-to-the-grave pattern of peasant life. Then we wouldn't be able to help them at all."

Garden Club and Hospital Wing nodded again, but Penelope and the stranger shared a look.

From her tall chair, Doña Elena suddenly clapped her hands. "Everyone, please! Señor Molina has a new idea. You all must hear it."

"Salud, salud, salud," called Jasper from his cage above their heads.

The room quieted, and Molina seemed to shrink an inch or two.

"Ah, Doñas, please," he said. "You embarrass me. I was just trying to say that sometimes—present company excluded, of course!—but sometimes older people are difficult to be around. And babies, who smile at everyone, need so much care. So, at the Centro para Bebes y Ancianos, the elderly will enjoy their final days looking after infants."

Doña Elena sipped her drink. Penelope watched Mrs. Slater move across the room to stand next to Mrs. Clancy, both of them visibly bristling with a sense of competition as they listened to the new proposal.

"But where will the infants come from?" Doña Anita asked.

"The orphanage, and perhaps others will be dropped off by their busy mothers."

"Will there be training?" she asked. "Will there be a test of competency and strength?"

"What we are asking," said Doña Elena, "is whether this idea seems safe to you?"

"Ah. And I would answer that risk is everywhere and merely seems large when we contemplate something new."

"And these oldest citizens, they would be women and men?"

Señor Molina looked confused. "Women are the natural caretakers of babies, Doña."

Doña Elena smiled. "But men also grow old and unpleasant to be around. Are you not concerned for them?"

"But the men will have no prior experience, Doña."

"Neither do I, Señor Molina. Did you imagine that you and the other old men of Fonseca would stroll and read papers all day in the Alameda Zaragoza while all the old women change diapers?"

He had no answer for this.

Doña Elena clapped her hands again. "Clearly there are one or two points that need developing. Meanwhile, let's have another pink gin for the babies."

"There is another caller waiting outside," Chela said. "He would like an audience."

"Why don't you let him come in?"

"He is a mariachi."

Doña Elena shook her head. "I don't understand the mariachi."

"That is why he is outside. Appreciation comes with time, Doña."

"I have been here sixty-six years."

"You are not musical," Doña Anita said.

Doña Elena gave her her blackest stare. "You know that is not true. I love Los Panchos." She put a hand to her heart at the thought of the singing group. "'Una aventura más'? That is beautiful singing."

Mr. Tuttle agreed. "Ah, Mexico. Land of tenors."

"I will not apologize for being startled by the grito."

"A spontaneous expression of lust or heartbreak is not for everyone," Chela said. It was meant as a challenge, and Doña Elena was considering it, but the confident stranger stepped forward and the moment for the mariachi was lost.

"If I could have your attention for a moment. I'd like to thank the Doñas for their gracious hospitality and introduce myself. My name . . ." He paused for effect, and it worked. His timing was excellent. "My name is Ernest Delaney."

Gasps sounded from every corner of the room. There was a general din of shuffling and scooting of furniture. Violet Slater and Rose Clancy went ashen. When the room was relatively quiet again, the stranger explained he was a distant relative from a branch of the family that emigrated from Ireland to New York when the other Delaneys aimed at the northern silver mines of Mexico.

The Doñas were intrigued, but skeptical. "Well, welcome to Mirando, Mr. Delaney. I'm sure you understand if we have some questions?"

"Of course."

Doña Elena started. She named a number of impossibly small towns in Ireland. He knew them all. Doña Anita quizzed him on the family tree. He passed. And then, when he mentioned having had a meal years ago with William in Monterrey, Chela stepped forward. What did William eat, she wanted to know. "When Don Guillermo went to Monterrey, he ate only one thing."

The Delaney met her eyes and bowed. "He had huevos rancheros and said they were never as good as yours."

Penelope had not seen Chela blush and would have said it was impossible.

The stranger turned to the room. "William Delaney was a man of integrity and law," he said. "He promoted commerce in the whole region. Fonseca would not be what it is today without his personality and business vision."

Penelope knew as much from the pink library.

"Ernest," Doña Elena said thoughtfully.

It struck Penelope as a little on the nose.

"From my mother," he said with a bow. "A prayer on her part, I'm sure. I've done my best to make her proud, God rest her soul." And here he took from his pocket a folded photograph, no bigger than a bank note. "May I?" he said, gesturing at the ofrenda.

"Of course! Please!" But they had to see her first. The crease in the photograph fell across the woman's face (convenient, thought Penelope), but the Doñas agreed her likeness was remarkably similar to their great-aunt Noreen of Moneymore, County Londonderry. He set it on the ofrenda, lit a candle, and bowed his head.

The Doñas were captivated. Penelope was amused. Mr. Azuela, Señor Molina, Mrs. Clancy, Mrs. Slater—all of them!—were very quiet.

"How many settings for dinner?" Chela asked loudly, visibly irritated by the arrival of the fine-looking stranger who had put her behind schedule.

"You'll join us this evening, Mr. Delaney?" Doña Anita asked.

He made another bow. He really was very good at them. "That is kind of you."

So the handsome stranger enters the fairy tale, Penelope said to herself. After dinner, the Delaney was given the room next to the Tuttles.

·· *Ghosts* ··

In Fonseca, Penelope woke up at half past two every night. At first she thought it was just the awkwardness of sleeping on the chaise. But she was also aware of creaks and taps too steady to be attributed to an old house. Perhaps Pax was making nighttime rounds. He was large enough to produce the sounds she heard, made strong by the fish heads and chicken livers Chela fed him in the kitchen. He was one of the finest felines Penelope had ever seen, with a shiny black coat and green eyes. Perhaps he wanted a warm spot at the foot of someone's bed. The next night when the sounds woke her, she got up from the chaise and opened the door. She wasn't so naive to think it wouldn't take some coaxing. Pax was like all his species, skeptical and reluctant to do anything wanted of him. What Penelope did not expect was to feel the cold of the library again, Pax nowhere to be seen.

"Hello?" she said, stepping out of the room and closing the door behind her so as not to wake Valpy. The tapping stopped and then broke out again, this time from the other end of the hallway.

This was not her first experience with the supernatural, and Penelope was not scared. There'd been a poltergeist at Squires Mount with whom she'd established reasonable terms after several incidents with the sinks. But a burst of furious tapping from both ends of the hall simultaneously startled her enough to jump back into the room and close the door.

The next day she brought the question to Doña Elena, who was in the morning room. This was where she wrote her letters, went over accounts, and nursed her worst hangovers. It was an unusually warm day for November, and several flies buzzed against the windowpanes. Seeing Penelope staring at them, Doña Elena said, "Mice frequently die in the walls. Pax is useless."

Penelope thought it best to get right to the point. "Is Mirando haunted?"

Doña Elena was not surprised by the question. "Oh, I'm not afraid of ghosts," she said. "They've always been very kind to me."

"I didn't say I was afraid."

"Just last night I saw a woman at the foot of my bed, huddled there, wrapped in a serape of unusual colors. She was cold, so cold. She looked like my mother, but she always ran hot."

"I've had similar experiences, but this was different."

"How?"

"It was louder."

Doña Elena tilted her head, considering. "Aren't all houses haunted? By snippets of conversation, indelible expressions, postures of the people who have passed through them? The only difference is how welcome we find it. The other day I saw a friend of my youth in the sloped shoulders of Mr. Flatley as he left the library. For a time we had a haunting every Thursday. Whether it was our old piano teacher or the bank manager before this one, we never knew. Both used to come on Thursdays, and both had a heavy footfall."

"This was a fierce tapping."

Penelope was certain she noticed a glint of recognition in the Doña's eyes, but just then one of the very fat, very black flies left the window and buzzed straight toward her. Penelope ducked, and the insect barely missed her forehead.

"Don't worry," the Doña said, returning to her letters. "Flies are dirty, but they are also a symbol of persistence and perseverance. I'd say that was a good sign for you."

Hoping for some—any—insight, and also to fortify herself and Valpy against Chela's stories, Penelope spent a day in the State Public Library, a building inspired by the Parthenon but, in a startling shift, made of pink stone. She learned that Fonseca was captured by American forces during the Mexican-American War. When the Mexican army tried to retake it, General Santa Anna attacked on George Washington's birthday, unwittingly inspiring the US troops. This was the sad anniversary of February 22, when the streets ran with tears. After terrible losses the Mexicans retreated, but General Taylor did not pursue them. He remained in Fonseca, and everyone knew why. The view was legendary: jasmine and jacaranda and climbing geranium everywhere. It was said there were as many natural springs as days of the year. The blue-stained mountains of the Sierra Madre set off the pale adobe skyline of the town, and in the evening swallows and starlings flew in bunting swoops. The murmurations were believed to predict the future; girls saw interlocked rings the night before they became engaged to their true loves.

In the reading room, Penelope shook her head. Even in the library, stories and facts in Fonseca were hard to separate.

About the Delaneys, Penelope learned that their ancestor Kerr Delaney had been a San Patricio, Irish soldiers who emigrated to fight for the United States in the Mexican-American War, but switched sides after growing disillusioned with the US Army's treatment of Catholic recruits, who, among other things, were forced to attend Protestant services. The San Patricios played a decisive role in several battles, and General Santa Anna said with a few hundred more like them, he could have won the war. Those not hanged never left Mexico.

Kerr's son, William, settled in Fonseca and quickly became a local hero. A very successful businessman, he gave the town a railway, a silver mine, a bank, and a guild hall. Penelope found William and Helen O'Sullivan's 1874 wedding announcement and notices of attendance at charity balls, library galas, museum benefits, and other festivities in the last part of the century. In 1899 William began construction on what was to be his masterpiece, the residence he called Mirando. He died before it was completed, but his son, also William, finished it before his own death in 1920. The second William Delaney was survived by his wife, Anita, and two sisters, Elena and Lucy.

## ·· *First Sunday of Advent* ··

Sunday, November 30, was the beginning of the season of waiting and preparation, and Chela spent the day placing poinsettias. They began arriving in the morning, a dozen at a time, all red, some gifts from friends or Pretenders, the rest the Doñas' annual order for Mirando. The flower was their favorite, having learned the legend of Pepita and "The Flowers of the Holy Night" as children. Pepita, a poor little girl living in a small town, made a bouquet of weeds and set it down by the crèche, the nacimiento, in her church on Christmas Eve. The angels, pitying her and her simple gift, transformed it overnight into the beautiful red flowers.

Doña Elena told the story at dinner one night to some confusion.

"You are thinking of the first Christmas Eve, in Bethlehem?" Mr. Tuttle asked.

"No, you are thinking of the little drummer boy," said Mr. Flatley.

Penelope and the Delaney exchanged a glance, an event that after a week she was beginning to anticipate, even enjoy. He was always looking in her direction to check her thoughts.

"Yes," agreed Doña Elena. "That's right. Our Pepita's story is less presumptuous."

"But the flower is native throughout Mexico," Mr. Flatley added. "Wouldn't the angels—"

Doña Anita dropped her fork, startling the table and ending the discussion.

By evening, poinsettias filled every corner of Mirando. The bright foil-wrapped pots lined both sides of the center staircase, just as the marigolds had done before them, and a lane led through the antechamber into the drawing room. There were five on top of the piano and a few nestled among the silver on the mantel. Several off-color interlopers were going to be sent back, but Valpy asked if he could have them. He brought one to Jesús, one to the nuns, and took the last up to their room. It was neither pink nor red, but a sort of sickly salmon.

"It will have to be watered," Penelope warned.

"I don't mind," Valpy said.

The arrival of the plants was undeniably festive and cheered the household. Chela set candles around the house as well, and there was word that a Christmas tree might be ordered. They were largely imported from Europe and expensive; Mirando had not had one in several years, but the Doñas thought it might be nice with a young boy staying. As the Doñas had hardly seen or spoken with Valpy since their arrival, Penelope thought it encouraging that they would do something so extravagant for his sake. Only

Pax, who nibbled the poinsettia leaves, was miserable. He knew from experience he would suffer from excessive drooling until Epiphany.

On Monday, after leaving Valpy with the nuns, Penelope found herself drawn to the Lady Chapel in the Church of San Esteban. If there'd been an Anglican church nearby, she would have walked herself there, as she did in Hampstead, but to the best of her knowledge, there wasn't one in the Zona Centro. Father Bedoya had told her the diocese of Fonseca was 98.9 percent Catholic. She'd been told there was an English chaplaincy, but, like the mountains, it was far away. The Reverend Fred Watson came into Fonseca from time to time. She was sure to run into him, she'd been told, but she hadn't. There were 48 Catholic priests in the diocese, which meant 8,958 Catholics per priest, the smallest ratio at any time since the founding of Fonseca. Father Bedoya was very proud of this.

The Lady Chapel was decorated in blue for Advent, Mary often depicted in blue to symbolize being full of serenity, wisdom, and grace. Penelope felt drawn toward the color after the discussion with the Hoppers. That was what she told herself, anyway, to explain her lingering at the threshold. It was also true that she did occasionally feel she might like to fold into her faith a greater reverence for Mary, but all the rest of the saints—and certainly the papacy—troubled her.

Advent is a powerful season and suddenly—ah! How she hated the suddenlys of Fonseca! They threw otherwise perfectly plausible events into a magical haze. But suddenly she was overcome by a desire to light a candle for her mother, a sentimental practice she did not particularly believe in. And yet, as the flame took, she felt her throat grow tight. To distract herself, she lit another for Tina. Then, feeling guilty, deciding that having started this she might as well get on with it, she added one for Valpy and her mother-in-law. But she couldn't include her mother-in-law and not her husband, so she lit one for Desmond as well.

His last letter had been full of news. Muriel Spark had responded to Allen Tate's essay, "The Man of Letters in the Modern World," from their October issue. Her letter—"VERY long," Desmond wrote—argued that the controlling theme of all good writing in their time was virtue. He said it was wordy and repetitive and he'd had a hard time following it, but thought it was probably good enough to print. He did like the line "I have heard it said that writers today do in fact live virtuously, because they cannot afford to do otherwise."

Desmond's letter was delightful until the paragraph about his new plan for cutting down.

"The idea is to have your first drink ten minutes later than usual. Then the next day ten minutes after that, and so on until you reach a time when it is simply too late to have a drink. It may be hard in the beginning, but I'm sure every day will be a little easier."

It sounded ridiculous to her, hopeless. It made her want to blow out the candle, but instead she lit another, for herself, for strength.

She tried to pray. "Our Father who art in Heaven whatever am I doing in Fonseca hallowed be thy name thy kingdom come thy will be done poor Desmond on earth as it is in heaven. Give us this day our daily bread with a little luck so much could be easier and forgive us our trespasses as we forgive those who trespass against us I do hope Valpy is okay and lead us not into temptation so hard with Mrs. Clancy but deliver us from evil Mrs. Slater for thine is the kingdom and the power and the glory forever and ever amen."

She began again to see if she could get it a little clearer, but it was no better the second time. She added a simple prayer of gratitude for the story she had begun in the red notebook. Then, looking at her row of candles, she wondered if it was doctrinally correct to light candles for the living. She glanced around, but there were no instructions and no one in the chapel to ask. She looked to the nave, but there were only a few people sitting in pews, heads bowed. She turned back to her little lights, leaned over, and quickly blew them all out, accidentally extinguishing several nearby at the same time. She stared in horror, imagining all the prayers she had just snuffed out. She was so horrified all she could do was scurry away.

That evening on her way down to the drawing room, Penelope ran into the Delaney on the first floor. He was standing at a window, very still, looking at the sky. She came up beside him and saw that he was watching birds flying over Mirando, a dozen at a time, all in the same direction.

"What are they?" she asked.

"Swallows. On their way to the cliffs of the Sierra Madre for the night."

"Farther than they seem," Penelope and the Delaney said at exactly the same time.

# DECEMBER

## The Hoppers

For days Valpy begged to go back to the Hotel Arizpe, and when Penelope finally relented, the Hoppers were indeed there and Jo was as good as her word. She greeted them warmly, invited them to join their table, and looked eagerly through Valpy's notebook. She praised Penelope for encouraging his drawing, and Penelope shared that it ran in the family. She also liked to draw and learned from her father, who illustrated a family magazine he made with his brothers for years.

"A family magazine! Can you imagine, Eddie?"

Edward was quieter, less interested in Valpy's pictures but not unkind. About one he said simply, "That's quite good." Jo looked pleased at this and patted Valpy's arm. The drawing was of the desk in their room at Mirando with the window above it.

"And where is this?" Jo asked about another one.

"That was our house in London, but we don't live there anymore." He flipped several pages to show her Chestnut Lodge.

"I like the other one better," Jo said.

"So do I," said Valpy.

Later Penelope explained to Valpy that Edward was a famous American painter. The Whitney Museum of American Art had had a retrospective of his work two years earlier. It was very unlikely, nice as Jo was, that Valpy would be invited to paint with them on the roof. So when Valpy returned the next afternoon announcing that he had an invitation to do just that, Penelope was dubious.

"How did this happen? Did Chela have something to do with it?"

She did not. He'd simply run into them with the nuns on Victoria Street, in front of the theater.

"The nuns took you to see a film?"

"Oh no. We were returning from a field trip to the Ojo de Agua, the oldest spring in Fonseca. The water eye," he translated for her.

"I know what it means," she said.

"The parish is small but devoted. Chela says their stations of the cross are the most strenuous."

"Valpy, tell me about the Hoppers."

"Mr. Hopper likes to see films when he's not working well, and Mrs. Hopper invited me to come paint with them. She said it would do them both good."

So a pleasant surprise was to find themselves now in the Hoppers' rooms at Guajardo House looking at mountains, not the real Sierra Madre, but the ones in an unfinished watercolor of Edward's. The shock was to find Violet Slater also there.

"Mrs. Fitzgerald," she said. "My goodness. How are you?"

This wasn't a real question. Penelope had known other Americans when she worked at the BBC during the war. She didn't try to answer.

Violet Slater had met the Hoppers a week earlier, introduced by a friend "who was surprised we didn't already know each other," she said, smiling at Edward.

Jo moved Edward toward the window before he could say anything in response. A row of dark clouds was moving at speed across the sky. "Why don't you keep your eye on those clouds and see if it looks like rain." She came back to Edward's watercolor, which was of the dome of San Esteban as seen from the rooftop where the Hoppers painted. "He's been trying to get San Esteban since the last time we were here, in forty-six," Jo explained. "Now he thinks the weather is against him. Every day just as he starts to like the light, the clouds come."

Valpy went to the window too. Holding his notebook to his chest, he stood with Edward looking anxiously at the sky.

"I haven't got the right blue for the mountains," Edward said.

Penelope would have said something about the texture was off, but now she studied the color. The mountains had gray, violet, purple, and brown layered wash over wash, heaviest in the shadows. In contrast, the sunbaked buildings hummed with heat in cream and yellow and peach. The picture was all sun and surfaces, no weather, no people, no sound. Penelope marveled at how completely Edward had edited out the humanity.

"Goethe wrote that we love to contemplate blue not because it advances to us, but because it draws us after it. That's the blue I need."

"We've looked everywhere," Jo said.

Penelope pointed to a lonely little door in the lower right of a hot white wall.

"Oh, yes," Jo said. "The door. He added that when I asked where all the people were. Apparently they're behind this little door, locked away tight."

In reality, the door did not exist in the south wall of San Esteban. From roof to ground the wall was a deep rose stucco, but Edward had made it mostly white, perhaps to set off the bright red, blue, and yellow of the dome.

"They are ruining the city," Edward said from the window. He gestured toward a building site across the street from San Esteban through which it was currently possible to see the mountains beyond town, but when the building was done, the view would be much constricted. It was one of many sites under construction in town.

"I believe that is one of my husband's projects," Violet said, squinting at the scaffolding.

"Is it?" Jo said cheerfully. "What's it going to be?"

"The new headquarters for Clancy Insurance."

As polite as she was, Jo missed a beat. "I don't think we've met your husband," she said.

Penelope gave all her attention to the painting; Valpy was still clutching his notebook, hoping they would make it out onto the roof, though that seemed more and more unlikely.

"Steve is from New York," Violet said. "His family is in real estate, among other things, and he studied engineering."

"Steve Slater," Edward said. "Sounds like a piece of machinery."

"And what brought you to Fonseca?" Jo said quickly.

"The Slater firm is expanding. In fact, that is something I wanted to talk to you about. I think I've mentioned that I'm interested in establishing an arts center in town, and I'd love for you to be involved." She turned to Edward. "Have you ever done a mural?"

"No, I have never *done* a mural," Edward barked.

Even Jo didn't know how to smooth this over, but just then the rain arrived with a thunderclap. "Ha!" Edward cried. "And now it's against all of you, too."

"Oh, stop," Jo said. "The rain is against no one." She went to the window and put her arm around Valpy's small shoulders. "You will come back another time." She showed them to the door, but before they were out, Violet spoke again, brave or oblivious, Penelope wasn't sure which.

"If a mural is too much, perhaps he'll donate a painting?"

"Oh, I doubt it," Jo said with a smile.

PENELOPE CONTINUED TO wake at half past two, but without incident, until one night she again felt the cold of the library and heard the tapping, which seemed this time to be right outside their door. She turned her head to look at Valpy, who was sleeping peacefully.

When the tapping didn't stop, Penelope sat up on the chaise. She hesitated only briefly, then stepped quickly to the door and tried to open it. Something seemed to be pulling it closed from the far side.

"I'm not afraid," she said.

The tapping increased. "Lucy?" she whispered.

## ·· *Chela* ··

The next day, Penelope found Valpy kicking his feet in front of Mirando. "All my yesterdays have lighted fools," he said, followed by a kick. "All my yesterdays have lighted fools." He hopped and stomped. She would have asked him what he was doing, but she knew the games of children were not always meant to be understood by adults.

She worried, too, that he had a lot on his mind. The nuns had announced a special Rosary to be said every morning until Valpy's return to England. The Mother Superior wrote it herself: "Heart of Jesús, grant that the eyes of Valpy's non-Catholic mother may be opened, that her tepid soul may become fervent, and that she may return to all her children in her rightful home. Amen."

Penelope told him she would talk to the Mother Superior.

"I don't think that's a good idea," he'd said.

"Why not?"

"There will be more prayers if she finds out a baby is coming."

Now he brought his strange recitation game to an end with two hops and a kick and looked up. "Chela told me a joke yesterday. Can I tell it to you?"

"Is it long? Does it make sense?"

"I think so. Why is consideration so heavy?"

"I don't know. Why?"

"Because everything is under it."

"Valpy, we should find some other children for you to play with."

"I like the kitchen. Do you know what *borracha* means?"

Penelope had an idea. She'd heard Chela say it under her breath when restocking the drink cart. "Do you?" she asked.

"It means drunk. But you can also say *bebida* or *beoda*."

"I see. And that line you were repeating before? Did Chela tell you that too?"

"No, that was Mr. Flatley. I have to recite it two hundred times for breaking his glasses. Then he'll tell me how it ends."

Penelope went to see Chela first. Her kitchen was a room of great industry and organization, and Penelope admired it. She knew she would never run anything as well. It smelled of Mexican and Irish spices: oregano, cumin, and cayenne, but also rosemary and sage. Chela had come to Mirando thirty years earlier, when William was still alive, and learned to make some of his favorite dishes. It was natural, people said, because she was also a descendant of a San Patricio; this explained her dark-blue eyes. She made Irish boxty with masa harina and Irish stew with dark-red mole. She made beef and cabbage with onion, garlic, tomatoes, and chiles,

Chiapas style. The Delaneys never asked for this culinary fusion, and indeed, sometimes they objected—the Doñas had never cared for her green chile scones—but Chela was not discouraged. Her shelves were lined with jars and pots, there were a great many cabinets from floor to ceiling, and her herbs grew in a garden box in the sunny window by the deep sink.

Chela held up a spoon, halting Penelope in the doorway. "The mole requires my attention." There were four large pots simmering on the wide black stove. The kitchen clock was secured on the wall above. It was orange, the color of marigolds, with a white face, bold numbers, and a surprisingly loud ticktock, louder than the grandfather clock in the front hall.

Chela put down her spoon and turned. "You are expecting a baby."

It did not surprise Penelope that Chela knew, only that she hadn't said something sooner. Penelope had been at Mirando over a month. She'd let out her skirt and found a loose-fitting dress at the mercado. This pregnancy, as compared to her others, she felt foggy, out of it, a little irresponsible. She'd found herself close to tears on several occasions, which was not characteristic. On the other hand, she was laughing more frequently.

"That is why you only pretend to sip your sherry," Chela said. "April?"

"Probably. Yes."

"Come." Chela turned down the radio and pulled a chair out from a corner. "If you aren't feeling well, the baby is a girl. It is the longer hair tickling the mother's gullet, though a spoonful of olive oil can help with that." Chela indicated the bottle of olive oil on the shelf, but Penelope declined. "If wide all around, a girl." She looked at Penelope again and tipped her head quickly left and right, uncertain. Penelope carried small. "I think, girl. If you smell lemons in the morning, a boy. Lemons at night, a girl."

"All I smell is marigolds. Morning, noon, and night."

"That's not possible."

"I'm telling the truth. I wish I weren't."

Chela sniffed and pursed her lips. "Perhaps if you had not come on Día de los Muertos. Your mother is deceased. Are you also dreaming of her?"

Penelope did not even try to resist the logic.

"What was her name?" Chela asked.

"Christina." Penelope cleared her throat. "What I came about is that I think Valpy needs the company of other children. The nuns are difficult and—"

"And you think I can help? With all I have to do in the kitchen?"

"I only thought you might have an idea or two."

"Talk to Señor Reynoso."

"I don't know who that is."

"He is gallant and kind, a veteran of the Mexican Revolution. His scouts are naturalists and navigators of the highest order. They informed Doña Lopez that the spring behind her house was flooding last Pentecost."

"Couldn't she see it for herself?"

"Doña Lopez has been blind for three decades."

"That is why she can smell the bread in the mornings!" Penelope exclaimed, delighted to have solved one of the Chela mysteries.

Chela shrugged. "They are good boys. Their headquarters is a bench in the Alameda Zaragoza."

Penelope knew another question would clarify nothing, so she was quiet for a time, watching Chela cook.

"I will put some cold vermouth on the cart for you. It will be next to a small green glass that you can use each night." It was a concession to extra work, and from Chela that was a gift.

"Thank you. A glass of something does seem to make things better for about five minutes."

Chela was stirring the mole and didn't reply.

"I appreciate you teaching Valpy some Spanish," Penelope continued, "but I came to object to some of the vocabulary you've given him."

Chela continued to stir quietly. Penelope tried to remember another time she had so little to say.

"He is very young, and on this trip there have been some difficult experiences."

"You are referring to the bus ride?"

"Oh. The bus ride was difficult, yes. But also, well, some things about Mirando."

"What don't you want him to understand?"

"Maybe it's not understanding so much as comparing."

"What don't you want him to compare?"

Suddenly, Penelope smelled the L'Heure Bleue. But how? She'd never worn it. She lifted her wrist to her nose to check.

Chela took one of her pots off the stove. Penelope, disoriented, stood and fiddled with a couple of knives crossed on the counter near her, but Chela stopped her hand. "They are keeping the rain away."

Penelope stared at the knives. "I do not understand Fonseca," she said.

"You've only been here a short time. Wait a little. *Espera un poco*. But waiting is hard. Perhaps the hardest thing."

Later Penelope checked the L'Heure Bleue box. According to the description, the top notes were aniseed and fresh bergamot, gently leading to rose, carnation, tuberose, and violet over a base of vanilla. Of course! That was why she thought she smelled it. Chela often used aniseed and vanilla in her desserts. What Penelope couldn't be sure of was whether Chela was magic, or whether she, Penelope, was just intimidated by one so competent.

·· *Letters* ··

In early December a batch of letters arrived from home. Penelope's neighbor Mathilda Wilson wrote to say there'd been a deadly fog in London. Penelope had to read the sentence twice and assumed Mathilda was exaggerating—this was a woman, after all, who kept all the family shoes by the front door in a straight row; who knows what she would consider deadly—but a letter from Jean confirmed the disaster: thousands dead in London. Jean also told her that Desmond had been carried home from the Duke of Hamilton on two consecutive nights. Not the fog, Penelope knew, but a catastrophic failure of the pushing-back-the-first-drink plan. "You know there is more work for Desmond at Chambers should he need it. He only has to come in more often."

Desmond's next letter had a new plan for cutting down: he was going to have only one drink every night. "I think for me there is no two," he wrote. "But I think there is a time after the first when I could stop."

There is no *one*, she thought. If the definition of a healthy love is the ability to share your deepest fears, then by that measure, she and Desmond had a robust love. The problem was in solutions. They shared the fear that Desmond was drinking too much, but differed in what to do about it. And indeed, the large, sloped handwriting in his next letter suggested this plan had also failed. He responded to her news of the Delaney. "I'm reminded of that old idea that there are only two kinds of stories: someone goes on a journey and a stranger comes to town. It seems you are living both. Isn't that remarkable."

The next letter after that was clearly from the contrite morning hours, handwriting small and neat, full of hopes and plans. Now he had decided he would only drink Guinness. It was more filling, and he would stop sooner. Also, he'd got his brother to agree to write a review for the spring issue. "He says it may be that new one in the Batsford series: *The Smaller English House*. I don't know whether this is a dig at us or not, but I think we can count on him for a page, at least."

He mentioned that L'Heure Bleue was the new queen's favorite scent. He thought this was a nice coincidence. Was it reminding her of home? She could not bear to tell him she wasn't wearing it, but on a number of sorrowful occasions, Penelope had walked streets out of her way in London, chasing a whiff of something like the scent her mother had worn. She would not do this to her children. All children had enough painful, indelible memories without their mothers wearing scent.

Also in early December, Mr. Azuela traded his old blue suit for a new one, still blue, but brighter. In this new blue suit, he sought to expand his influence and began to drink level with the Doñas.

For years he had been giving his report faithfully at five o'clock, certain it was only a matter of time before the Doñas agreed with his view of the situation. The Doñas no longer owned the mine, but they liked to have news of it, as they had for years, and he liked to give them the news, as he had for years, and his father before him. In this way he reminded them of two things. One, that he still worked there. And two, that it was he, and all the Azuelas before him, who had made the mine what it was. If there was a legacy to give it was because of his family, and that was worth, if not the legacy itself, significant compensation.

In the beginning, Azuela saw the visiting hour as entertainment, two old women enjoying what they could in their waning years, but lately, particularly after the arrival of the English mother and son—and then the man calling himself a Delaney!—he had begun to worry.

The Doñas did not notice Azuela's new suit, but they did notice that he was drinking more, and the more he drank, the more upbeat and entertaining he became. He liked Los Panchos as much as they did, and sometimes after the third or fourth cocktail, all three sang along. "Una aventura más" was a favorite.

"*Yo sé queso,*" the Doñas sang in unison. Their voices were pleasant together. "*Una aventura más para ti.*"

Mr. Azuela had been singing along, too, but stopped suddenly. "What was that? Did you say, *Yo sé queso*?"

"I know," Doña Elena said. "I've never understood that line. The song is so beautiful, but why is he singing about cheese?"

Azuela's face sobered quickly. "He is not singing about cheese. It is *'Yo sé que soy.'* I know I am."

"I never thought that," said Doña Anita. "But my Spanish has always been better than yours."

Elena lifted her drink. "Well, it sounds like queso, and that means cheese."

## ·· *Detour* ··

A few mornings after her chat in the kitchen with Chela, Penelope and Valpy came downstairs to find the front hall filled with eleven- and twelve-year-old boys. They were Reynoso's scouts, they told her.

"You're real?" Penelope said. They were short and tall, light and dark, roughly split between sons of the Irish expat community and those native to Fonseca. All were serious of countenance and wearing orange jerseys.

A tall Mexican boy in a floppy sailing hat spoke. "Captain Reynoso told us to come and see if Valpy needed anything."

"Anything?" Valpy asked, starstruck.

"Mainly we have lanyards and torches. Do you need a torch?"

A torch was one of the few things Valpy had packed so that he could read at night. Both sides were briefly at a loss, but then the scout leader, Genaro, pushed his hat back and turned to Penelope.

"Can he throw, señora? We found a baseball yesterday, and Doña Lopez gave us a bat. Can he come to the park?"

To the best of her knowledge, Valpy had never thrown a baseball, but one look at his face told her she should not give him away. "Of course," she said. "This is very kind of you."

Genaro and the scouts returned Valpy two hours later happy and tired, with good color in his cheeks. Penelope felt overwhelmed with love for the scouts and wanted to give them something, but all she could do was wave them off at the door. Suddenly Chela stepped around her. "Come back tomorrow and you'll have churros," she called.

The boys beamed, saluted, and headed off in all directions.

"Chela. Thank you. Can I help?" Penelope asked.

"Ack, no! My apple churros are famous, and I make them alone."

And so Valpy began spending his afternoons with Reynoso's scouts, a positive balance to his mornings with the nuns. If they were still praying for her, she didn't know about it. The only downside was that scouting the calles of Fonseca was dusty work, and suddenly she had much more laundry to do. She didn't mind, though, because she'd always liked the warm atmosphere of a good launderette and the one on Calle Juan Aldama was just that. She began taking her notebook.

One afternoon she ran into the Delaney. She thought everyone at Mirando gave their washing to Chela, who gave it to Esperanza, her delicate young cousin, who often gave it to another cousin, but here the Delaney was doing his own just like her. Seeing him sitting quietly before the machine, book in hand, she stopped abruptly in the doorway with her bag.

Just then the Delaney's machine stopped, and in getting up to shift his clothes, he saw her and dropped his laundry powder. They stared at each other through the door until her cheeks felt warm.

What was she going to do? Find another launderette?

"Is Ernest really your name?" she asked when she was finally inside, seated next to him, their clothes spinning in washers side by side. Both of them were holding books. Neither was reading.

"Of course it is."

"What if I said I'm skeptical."

"I wouldn't be surprised."

"Is it common for people to doubt your given name?"

"No. I wouldn't be surprised if *you* doubted it. You're more discerning than most."

She looked down to hide her expression. "It is the Delaney part that matters, though, isn't it?"

"And why are you staying at Mirando, may I ask?"

"We were summoned."

The Delaney raised his eyebrows.

"The Doñas wrote to me of a family friendship. They wanted to meet Valpy."

"So I am competing with an eight-year-old?"

"He's six," Penelope said.

"Really? He seems older."

"That is true."

The Delaney shook his head. "And charming. It's an unfair fight."

"But surely you do not have to compete. You are family."

He nodded.

"You are from New York, you said. What do you do there?"

"Ah, no. I said my branch of the family went to New York originally. I was born and raised in New Jersey."

"What do you do?"

"My family owns a marketing company."

"I see. And how can you take so much time away?"

An old woman opened the door to the launderette, struggling with several large laundry bags. The Delaney leapt to her assistance. He had taken off his jacket, and as he stretched one arm over the woman's head to hold the door and reached with the other to take her bags, his thin linen shirt revealed the muscles of his back. The movement would have been awkward on anyone else.

"Let's just say my particular skills are not needed at the moment," he said when seated next to her again. The launderette was warm. He rolled up his shirtsleeves.

"Is there really a legacy?" Penelope asked.

"A sizable one. The Delaney silver mines were very lucrative before nationalization."

"I see." She shook her head. "You know, I am always saying that in Fonseca but I don't, really."

"I see," he said, and they both smiled. "Valpy has one disadvantage," the Delaney said after a moment.

"What is that?"

"An early bedtime."

She smiled again, and he turned toward her in his chair. She felt she had not understood a strong chin until now. Or, for that matter, the singular appeal of strong arms.

"And are you really a Penelope?"

She nodded.

"Weaver of stories." He held out his hand. "Well, now we're properly introduced."

Oh how much simpler life would be if it came with proper warnings, or if we could read the warnings we are given. At the front of the launderette, "Mar y cielo" played on the radio, the romantic sound of Los Panchos and their gentle requinto guitars. But the signs are not always clear, and so you stand up, fold the clothes, and leave the launderette. What you must do, Penelope believed as the Delaney held the door for her, was try your best to treat the situation as comedy.

Dear ——

I have been turning over the questions you ask in my mind and I will tell you what I can.

I don't remember her ever wearing any scent. But then you must remember throughout all my later childhood she was absolutely stony broke and there was no money for basics let alone luxuries.

She was a great list maker, usually on the backs of old envelopes or circulars that came through the door. And she also wrote notes to herself which I still find sometimes. I never saw her burn any of them, though. Much easier in Edwardian days when there was always a fire burning.

I am sure she wrote long detailed letters from Mexico and I am sure my father wrote back at equal length. They were both marvelous letter writers. How wonderful it would be to read them now. It was a marvelous moment when we discovered the letters she wrote to her mother when she was eighteen and staying in France, so funny and observant and illustrated with tiny pen and ink drawings.

She always drank extra dry vermouth as it was, no ice or lemon or tonic water. A couple of glasses before dinner in the evening if possible in her favorite small cut glass green tumbler which I still have. I don't know when this habit started, I'm afraid. Certainly she always asked me to stop for a large bottle when I picked her up from the station when she visited.

As regards her pregnancy, my mother was very reluctant to discuss any personal detail about anything and that includes pregnancy and childbirth. Remember that she came from a family where a cloak of silence was thrown over any suffering or distress. After her mother died she was never mentioned again by my grandfather for example, and when my uncle Rawle returned from a POW camp his ordeal was never talked about. However we know she had at least two miscarriages and possibly a stillbirth. I imagine she decided to set off for Mexico before she realized she was pregnant and then went anyway.

It is so hard to imagine on what basis she was staying there. Of course I wish I'd asked her, but she was an expert at avoiding any direct answers and we probably would be none the wiser.

My brother told me a very good story about climbing a pyramid in Mexico and forgetting their picnic which I am sure he will tell you. If not I'll give him a nudge.

With all best wishes,
Tina

·· *Chela* ··

Chela stood Valpy on a little stool at her kitchen counter. She gave him a mortar and pestle and showed him how to fill the mortar only one-third full. Sometimes he also helped sweep the floor, snip fresh herbs, and collect the eggs. "You are not the first child to help me in the kitchen," she said.

"Who was the first?"

"I won't tell you, but you will have to work hard to be as good." She added to his piles of coriander, sesame, and achiote seeds. "Pound and swirl, pound and swirl. Use the sides too. Was the bus ride interesting? Did you see some of America?"

"Yes. A woman in Tennessee told us we were having a big time."

"What does that mean?"

"I don't know."

"Was the bus full?"

"Sometimes."

"What did you see?"

He stopped his work. "At night I could only see the reflection of the people on the bus."

"Well, what kind of people were they? Americans traveling here and there?" She was making him hot cocoa, her champurrado.

"The people in front slept a lot, but the people in the back stayed awake."

"Why?"

"Mama said it's hard to sleep when you're worried."

Chela shook her head. "Don't go back that way." She lifted the pot from the stove and poured the drink into his unglazed mug. The mixture of chocolate, brown sugar, molasses, a little anise, thickened with masa, was the best thing he'd ever tasted.

"Now Spanish. Kitchen?"

"*La cocina.*"

"Riches?"

"*La riqueza.*"

"Luck?"

"*La suerte.*"

"Bueno!"

## ·· Second Sunday of Advent ··

The second Sunday of Advent, the guests of Mirando walked to Mass at San Esteban together. "En masse to Mass," Mr. Flatley said, delighting only himself. The Doñas took the lead, their black veils bobbing, one a bit straighter than the other. Then came Mr. Flatley, quietly observing the birds and the trees after no one had appreciated his wordplay. Next were the Tuttles, arm in arm, then Penelope and Valpy. The Delaney offered his arm to Chela, who usually attended San Ignacio on Calle Juan Aldama, but because of the looming Posadas had stayed over at Mirando the night before.

After the launderette, the Delaney had given Valpy a set of drawing pencils. He'd begun waiting for Penelope to go into the drawing room, and they'd started a game of lifting their glasses every time Mr. Flatley began a sentence, "You are thinking of . . ."

"What are your motives?" she'd asked him. "Am I playing some part in your strategy at Mirando?"

"You are thinking I'm a con man." He'd smiled and lifted his glass. "I'm offended."

She'd lifted hers, too, but did not say she hadn't been thinking that.

Penelope was familiar with the Latin Mass from having attended services in Hampstead with Desmond. She was delighted to see the responsorial psalm was Psalm 90, one of her mother's favorites. But each time the congregation recited the first line, "Lord, you have been our dwelling place in all generations," Penelope only heard *dwelling place*. The rent at Chestnut Lodge was due.

The bishop was visiting, which might have explained the excessive incense, and his homily, in Spanish, was about waiting. Sitting next to Penelope, Chela leaned over now and then to give whispered updates: "He is comparing the peaceful waiting that is the season of Advent to the waiting of the workers on street corners for day jobs at the grand haciendas."

Penelope had seen them. They gathered early, chatted pleasantly, sipped from thermoses, and carried packed lunches. One by one the trucks came, taking two or three at a time until the corners were empty.

Chela leaned in again. "He says the US government airlifted thousands of immigrants back to Mexico this year, but the program has run out of money. The Mexican government was offering train rides, but now this program has also run out of money. Both economies are thriving. You'd think somebody could figure this out." She looked at Penelope. "I said that, not him."

Just then a ray of sunlight penetrating a green meadow of

stained glass far above the bishop's head turned him a sickly green. The ray became a dusty cylinder engulfing Bishop Barragán's head. There was blue in the light, too, and Penelope thought of Edward's painting.

The collect of the day was for the workers: "Almighty God, who has so linked our lives one with another that all we do affecteth, for good or ill, all other lives: So guide us in the work we do, that we may do it not for self alone, but for the common good; and, as we seek a proper return for our own labor, make us mindful of the rightful aspirations of other workers, and arouse our concern for those who are out of work."

Chela leaned over. "Doña Lopez has a boarder recently returned from America." She shook her head and crossed herself. "He is a master carpenter, but his wages are too low. In the off months, he must follow the rhythms of the harvest, picking grapes, oranges. Some have died of dehydration in a town with as many springs as days of the year!" She crossed herself again.

The nuns brought the children in after the profession of faith. All were clutching their second-Sunday-of-Advent craft, and the sound of several dozen white construction paper doves rustled in the aisles. The children found their families, the doves were pinned down in the pews, and the liturgy of the Eucharist began. Classical theologians had concluded that a Mass could be fully realized at thirty minutes. At San Esteban, it never ran shorter than ninety.

After church Doña Anita announced she was retiring to her room and would not be down for some time.

"The last time you said this," said Doña Elena, "we didn't see you for a week."

"You have all your visitors to keep you company." Anita turned and slowly climbed the stairs.

Later, Penelope offered to take up her tea. She wanted to help, of course, but it did occur to her that it was also an opportunity for Valpy to spend time with one of the Doñas alone.

She and Valpy collected the tray in the kitchen from Chela, but when they were in the passage outside the Doña's door, Anita called out, "Don't come in!" It was a command to stop them in their tracks, and it did. She never spoke so forcefully in the drawing room.

"It is Penelope, Doña. And Valpy. We have your tea?"

"Why didn't Chela bring it?"

Penelope looked at Valpy. "She is busy with the preparations for Las Posadas, Doña," he said.

"She is? Who says we are participating this year?"

He did not know the answer. They heard a rustling, a struggle with blankets, bedsprings creaking. "Fine," Doña Anita said. "Come in."

She was sitting up in a high double bed against a bank of pillows looking quite well, her cheeks rosier than they often were downstairs. The room was large but sparsely furnished. There was a white-painted cabinet and dressing table with muslin cover. A stack of books had toppled over on the floor near the bed, and a Victrola, her own, for Elena controlled the one in the drawing room, had a shelf of records next to it. A sewing machine stood in one corner and a tall, surprisingly healthy camellia in the other. When she saw them looking at it, she said, "A sturdy houseplant is a great comfort."

Doña Anita's thoughts were transparent across her face. It was one of the things Penelope liked about her. Doña Elena's face was composed and rarely revealed anything.

"How is Pax?" Anita asked. "Have you seen him? Will you make sure Doña Elena is kind to him? She despises him for loving me more." Every night, Pax howled in the early dawn hours until Anita called for him and the haunting sound stopped. "How can I help who he loves?" Anita said. Her legs were restless under the sheets, and she pressed them with her hands. "You know she didn't even come to the wedding?"

"Your wedding?" Penelope asked.

"Yes." It must have been years and years ago, but the hurt in the Doña's face was fresh. "Her own brother! Would one of you press on my legs? It helps."

Penelope helped Valpy up onto the high bed, and perhaps because he was no longer standing beside her and the Doña was lying down, she noticed her middle and gasped.

"Mrs. Fitzgerald! Are you—?"

"I am."

"But, when? How far along?" Valpy was sitting across her shins now, and her legs were quiet.

"Four and a half months."

"But you traveled so far! And you've been sightseeing!" Doña Anita cried.

"I feel very well. Better than when I arrived, actually."

"Mrs. Lopez had six months of bed rest with each of her children!" Doña Anita said.

"Is that the same Mrs. Lopez Chela knows?"

"She has two babies."

That didn't answer the question, but that wasn't unusual at Mirando. "Well, this is my third," Penelope said, "and all's well."

"This is not what Doña Elena wants," she said. "Not at all." Her eyes suddenly sparkled. "But I won't tell her if you won't."

"I didn't intend to keep it a secret."

"But you could. You might. You probably should. For as long as you can, at least. You can always blame Chela's cooking. She uses too much cheese."

"But why would Doña Elena mind?"

Doña Anita looked surprised. "Because she prefers to be the center of attention. Didn't you know?"

Penelope stood straighter and pulled her dress loose around her. Doña Anita nodded. "Yes, that's better. I can help, you know. I will be on your side."

The idea of sides, pitting the Doñas against each other, seemed like a very bad course. Penelope was also ashamed to admit that if it came to this, she was sorry to be aligned with the Doña who seemed less powerful, more fragile. She changed the subject. "I haven't had a chance to thank you for your letters, Doña Anita."

"What letters?"

It was Penelope's worst fear. "Your kind invitation to Valpy and me to come visit?"

"Oh, that was Elena. She felt the evenings were growing dull." The Doña's eyes widened. "But I don't mean to be rude! We have enjoyed having you. The house has been happier since you arrived." She looked at Valpy, still on her legs.

"Would you like someone to read to you?" he asked. "I like being read to when I'm sick."

"Oh, no thank you. I'm not sick. I just need a rest. I am a burden to Elena, and sometimes I need a break from her judgment. I'll come down soon. If I don't, I begin to brood all day. I start to hear every crash and shout, every tick and tock. And Elena will send me to the nerve home."

"Are you peaceful? Do you need anything?" Penelope asked.

"Peaceful? No. But I am patient. People assume peace and patience go together, but they don't have to. Not in my experience." She looked at Valpy. "You are a sweet boy, and the perfect weight, I must say. I wish I could give you something."

Penelope felt a surge of hope—even a small sum would help as she was going through their spending money faster than she'd anticipated and their debt was growing by the week. But the Doña flopped toward her bedside table drawer, fished around in it, and pulled out an old gilt medal, some sort of commemorative medallion.

She handed it to Valpy. "What is the date on it?"

"January 30, 1866," Valpy read. He and Penelope waited, but the date seemed to mean nothing to the Doña.

"January 30 is my birthday," Valpy offered.

The Doña's eyes widened. "Is it?"

"What does it mean?" Valpy asked.

"I don't know," she said.

Penelope told the Doña they would bring her tea again the next day. At the door, she adjusted her dress over her front, and Doña Anita caught her eye and nodded conspiratorially.

"Valpy, what are Las Posadas?" Penelope asked when they were out in the hall.

"Nine nights of neighborly processions from door to door. A local boy and girl play Joseph and Mary and ride donkeys. Chela thought I might be able to do it, but another boy was already chosen. The procession is refused twice, then the third house lets them in for a communal Rosary and refreshments. It's a lot of work for Chela."

"Will Esperanza help?" Penelope asked.

"As much as she ever does," Valpy said.

·· *The Serape* ··

When the Delaney gave Penelope a serape before an expected cold snap, Penelope, who hadn't had such a perfect gift, beautiful and useful, in so long, didn't trust herself to speak. She just held the blanket, admiring its color and pattern.

"You said you'd been cold," he said, and it was true. She had mentioned the cold, though not the tapping, and he'd remembered. That was the problem. He gave her his full attention, and attention was the purest form of generosity. It was also very attractive.

"I wanted a serape," she said. "But I didn't need one."

She must have looked sad, for he tried to reassure her. "It was on sale! Truly! It wasn't much."

But she didn't believe him. He had good taste, his own clothes were well made, and the serape was darker and more mysterious than the ones she had seen at the mercado. Most of those were in shades of red and orange, threaded with yellow or amber, but the serape from the Delaney used dark blues and greens; to her, the colors of endurance. Its weave was very fine and the design was unusual, a vertical mosaic for the field with a scalloped circle of the darkest blue, some deep purple, and a golden brown in the center. She loved everything about it.

The gift of the serape was on a Wednesday. The following Friday, the cold snap well under way, was the traditional beginning of Christmas, the night households all over Fonseca set up the nacimiento. Chela brought all the Christmas boxes into the drawing room, warning that Mirando was out of spirits until Jesús returned.

"How long will he be gone?" said Doña Elena.

"How can I know? He must go all the way to Lomas del Sur."

But Jesús returned that afternoon with two barrels of whiskey, a crate of gin, and a Christmas tree.

Chela invited the scouts to help set up the nacimiento and trim the tree, and they arrived with Señor Reynoso, every one of them scrubbed and dressed for a party. Quiet at first, Chela's champurrado warmed them up. There were many boxes of ornaments, far more than one tree, even one twice as tall as Jesús, could hold. They stood it up in the front hall, where the ceiling was two stories. The boys would use the staircase to reach the higher branches after unwrapping all the ornaments and deciding which ones they liked best.

"It is nice to have young voices in the house again," Chela said. She had pulled chairs from the drawing room out into the hall so the Doñas could watch the festivity. "Don't you think so? The patter of little, fast feet."

"Yes," Doña Anita agreed. She looked very happy.

Penelope, curious, couldn't resist. "You are referring to young visitors or family?" She was sorry to sound like Mr. Flatley.

"I'm not," said Chela.

"Pretty Jasper, salud, salud," called Jasper, lonely in the drawing room.

Doña Elena looked ill-tempered. "Tell the boys to be careful. The tiles are slippery."

The nacimiento was arranged under the tree, and the cast extended far beyond what Penelope and Valpy knew. There were the usual figures, of course, but also schoolteachers and farmers, milkmaids and bakers, jurists and revolucionarios. The extra roles extended to the animals too. There were elephants and camels, jackrabbits, jaguars, and parrots.

The infant Jesús was confoundingly large. Made of rough earthenware, he towered over the other miniatures, and Penelope watched as Valpy tried to figure out where to place him. She didn't know how to advise him. He certainly wasn't going to fit in the little manger before the much smaller Mary, Joseph, and blessed donkey who had carried them to Bethlehem.

Genaro explained the discrepancy. "What does it matter if he is bigger? After all, he is king of the whole world." He took the figure from Valpy and leaned him up against the back wall of the stable.

Penelope was glad to have a chance to thank Señor Reynoso for sending the scouts. He must have been her father's age, but was taller and more robust. He had a dark mustache and wore a short jacket over a suit vest in the Mexican style. The scouts, over whom he exerted a mysterious but direct influence, called him Captain and clearly adored him. When she told him how grateful she was for Valpy's sake, he refused to take any responsibility. "Some of the scouts have had lessons with the nuns of San Esteban. They were eager to help a fellow soul."

"Nevertheless, you must have encouraged them," she said. "In my experience older children don't always want to spend time with younger ones." Penelope had an older brother.

"The scouts all have younger siblings to whom they have been kind. It is one of the requirements. Valpy seems older."

"How long have you run the scouts?" she asked.

"These boys have been together three years. They run their own ship. I'm just their mentor because I grew up on the water in Tampico. They wanted to be sea scouts, you see, but in landlocked Fonseca that idea can only be taken so far."

Penelope liked him immediately for entertaining the idea at all and not crushing the boys' spirits. Señor Reynoso had a deep and sonorous voice. If Fonseca had had a large body of water for the boys to train on, Penelope had no doubt his voice would be well heard over the wind and the waves, instructing his scouts in the skills they needed for survival.

"Is there a lot to learn about seafaring without a boat?" she asked.

"They are making progress in meteorology, first aid, knot tying, and sailmaking. Of course we also focus on service and leadership skills, sports, and I try to throw in some mountaineering."

"Of course! You have the Sierra Madre."

"I would like to take the ship to the mountains this spring." He was the first person in Fonseca who had not told her they were farther than they seemed.

"Will you teach them any botany?" she asked.

"Of course. The wildflowers in the Sierra Madre are very special."

The tree decorating complete, the scouts were suddenly around Penelope.

"How long are you staying?"

"When do you leave?"

"Will you be here through Christmas?"

"Will you send us a Flyin-Saucer from America?"

They were all good questions. Penelope and Valpy hadn't been officially invited to spend Christmas at Mirando, but it was also true that she'd made no plans yet for their return. She latched on to the last question.

"A flying saucer?"

"It's a plastic disc for throwing long distances," Señor Reynoso explained. "Very popular in America. Apparently anyone can learn to throw one well." He was careful not to look at any of the scouts, but one or two of them shuffled awkwardly.

"They are not going back that way," Chela said. "And of course they are staying for Christmas. Valpy set up el nacimiento! It would be bad luck if he left now."

THAT NIGHT THERE WERE WHISKEY gingers, and Penelope wore the serape to the drawing room, partly because she was cold—Fonseca had had snow flurries in the afternoon—and partly because she was worried about Doña Elena discovering her condition. Doña Anita had come down from her room, but they didn't have a chance to keep their secret together very long.

"Where is that from?" Elena said immediately about the serape. "Is that one of ours? Let me see it? Where did you find it?"

Penelope froze. The Delaney wasn't down yet, but she did not intend to reveal it was a gift. "It's from the mercado, Doña. I've been looking for one since we arrived."

"Come here," she said. "There is black in the border. That's rare. I can't believe this is from the mercado. The dye comes from a wood only found in Brazil."

Penelope stepped a little closer to the Doña's chair and looked down at the border.

"Closer!" Elena said and grabbed at the serape, pulling it and Penelope's dress askew. "It must be from the Fonseca Serape Factory on Victoria Street."

"The one next to the Taxco Silver Factory?" Penelope asked, but it was hopeless. Elena had seen that she was expecting.

"I knew," Anita said, sly and proud.

"You hid your condition from me," Elena said.

"I didn't intend to, Doña. I just didn't announce it."

"But you told Doña Anita."

"I didn't. She noticed."

"I'm more observant, Elena," Anita said.

Doña Elena ignored this. "You came all this way with one child, carrying another, and left one behind. I don't know whether to admire or pity you. There is something showy about having a baby at Christmas, though."

"Good heavens," said the Delaney, arriving and trying to settle Penelope with the serape in a chair. "No one die at Easter."

"I am due in the spring, Doña," Penelope said.

"Well, poor Mrs. Slater. This time last year she was expecting a child. She's had a hard time, but she's remarkably resilient."

Penelope was grateful to Señor Molina for intervening just then with a new proposal: educational programming for the new televisions coming in. Penelope thought it was his best idea yet, but the Doñas did not. Chela restocked the cart, and the Delaney brought over Penelope's small green glass.

Dear ——

I remember the sisters as rather stiff old ladies, not the sort to hug you or give you sweets. I don't know if they took a particular interest in me, but even assuming they did, I would not have been aware of it. In those days little boys were supposed to be quiet and polite with adults—after all I called my own grandfathers "sir." Perhaps that is why I remember the servants in the garden and kitchen better, who were very kind to me.

I don't remember other visitors, and I don't recall the dinners because small boys weren't invited. More to your point, PM's essay is in my view essentially fictional both explicitly and implicitly in the changed names, etc. It is my belief that there were no other potential heirs there, let alone a suspicious death. It looks to me more like the seed of a mystery or detective story. Remember her own first novel was just this sort of thing, including an inheritance.

Returning to the real world, our research on the Purcell (not "Delaney") family indicates that there were direct heirs to the old man even though these sisters were spinsters. So, the inheritance does not appear to have been an issue at all.

A final thought—as you know, PM was always fascinated by ghost stories, and by the writing of M.R. James in particular. It would not surprise me if the somewhat spooky atmosphere of the house and its inhabitants put her in mind of these things.

Best wishes,
Valpy

## *Waiting*

She went to Fonseca to try for the legacy, but was there something else, another reason to embark on such a long and difficult trip? She was thirty-five years old, pregnant with her third child, married to a man who was a brilliant writer and editor, but who had begun to drink too much, too often. Not so different from many other men they knew, especially among those who had had a bad war. But his trajectory was off. He kept resolving to cut down and then failing to do so. Did she leave in order to decide if she could stay?

Why did the Doñas invite her? Why were they entertaining half of Fonseca every evening? For the spectacle and influence of it? The desire to preserve dignity in decline is powerful. But how long had this been going on? Months? Years? No one seemed to know when the legacy would be given, how it would be distributed, or even how big it was. Though it must have been very large. The northern silver mines had been successful for over a century.

At least Penelope finally got a chair. Chela ordered Mrs. Tuttle to return the one she'd apparently taken from their room before they arrived, and the same day Penelope walked up to Calle Juarez, where she bought more letter paper, envelopes, and a box of matches.

Back at Mirando, she sat down at the desk. She needed to write to Desmond. His last letter had said he was worried they were going to be short an article for the February issue.

"We have that feature on the 20th century renaissance of tapestry," he wrote, "and another poem by Donald Hall. It's rather brilliantly delicate about his break with a former love. I plan to go to the Royal Opera's 'Boris Godunov' on January 6 and will write about that for February. There should be time. What about you? Have you been able to see any art?"

He reported that Stevie was back up to seven novels for the March issue, one of them the new Faulkner, *Requiem for a Nun*. "Here's the first sentence for you: 'Mr. Faulkner's mind is an obsessive case history in violence and sex. But of course, being the artist he is, he uses his infirmities—positively feeds upon them, munching devoutly . . .' I won't go on. You get the idea. She likes his language, not his thought. She called it fulminous, cites white guilt feelings and American nation-consciousness. Oh dear."

Penelope started her reply with a lengthy description of the Zona Centro, and the small English-language bookshop on Victoria Street that had a friendly proprietress named Jenna from Ealing. "She doesn't carry *World Review* but I'm going to convince her." She told him about the Alameda Zaragoza, where she took

Valpy after his catechism class. He liked to watch the paddleboats navigating the lake the shape of Mexico, but was sometimes still under the nuns' influence. "Yesterday it was Matthew 6:25: 'Do not worry about your life, what you will eat or what you will drink, or about your body, what you will wear.' Valpy asked, 'But then why should we try the elotes? Why should we buy me a sombrero?' I told him it is because we are making memories and we are allowed to care about those. I hope you agree."

She did not tell Desmond that she'd argued with the Catholic priest, Father Bedoya. It had started innocently. He'd said she would enjoy Christmas in a Catholic country. She said she didn't believe it would be so very different. He said it was. She said it wasn't. He said it was. And at that point she realized they were arguing about something else, and so she said, "You know what I have always liked about our two religions is the common thread of charity," to which he'd pressed his lips together and said no more.

She did tell Desmond the Alameda Zaragoza was famously fifteen hundred steps long. Everyone mentioned it. "But whose steps, I ask, and so far no one has given me a satisfactory answer. The tutor Mr. Flatley is investigating whether a step has ever been a historical unit of measure, but I am not hopeful. He takes all the fun out of learning. He 'flattens' it Valpy said the other day! I was very proud of his wordplay. So was he."

The Hoppers were out on the rooftop, side by side. Today they didn't seem to be arguing. Penelope turned back to her letter and wrote with increasing speed. She told Desmond about the birds falling quiet when the Doñas walked to church, and how Valpy had begun an irrigation project with the gardener, Jesús. She wrote that it was odd to know a man with this name who was short-tempered, then she stopped. She knew very well what Desmond's response to all this would be. He'd already asked in his first letter when all she'd mentioned were Chela's rattling windows. "How is this real?"

To which she would very much like to have replied, I have no idea. I'm as baffled as you. She had lost track of how many times she'd said to herself since arriving, This can't be real. I've wandered into a yarn.

She told him that she would consider writing something for the journal. She'd like to see the murals of Rivera and Siqueiros if she could get to Mexico City, though she had no idea how she would arrange that. Lastly, she mentioned that a man named Delaney had arrived. "If this were a fairy tale, it would be hard to imagine a more perfect heir. He is intelligent, charming, and good-looking. He sings and plays the piano (the other night Liszt's 'Campanella'!) and although I have not seen him dance, I can imagine he does so quite well. He's a good storyteller, appears to have a sense of humor, and keeps his head in a room full of drunk people. Sometimes we are the only two. If what he says is true, and he is indeed related to the Doñas, Valpy and I should probably start packing our bags."

She made a small sketch of a vase of marigolds at the bottom, put the letter in an envelope, and sealed it.

Her notebook sat on the corner of the desk, still blank but for the list of Pretenders she'd started. She had been waiting to write something until things at Fonseca were clearer, just as she'd been waiting for Desmond to get back from the war, waiting until a child was born, waiting until they had more room in the house, waiting until they had more money, waiting until she finished yet another article to shore up the journal. That day in Fonseca, in her room at the top of Mirando, she decided to stop. She turned the notebook upside down, making the back the front, opened the cover, and began something new.

·· *The Bird Museum* ··

For weeks Señor Garza had not been well enough to attend visiting hour at Mirando, but he sent word via Chela that the English visitors would be very welcome to come see his bird museum. It was not yet a full-fledged museum, he apologized, more of a collection in his home. All the same, he brought visitors through as often as he could. He lived on the outskirts of Fonseca, and as Jesús was too busy to drive them, Penelope asked if Jo Hopper could bring them and see the museum too. Señor Garza was delighted; Edward was not. What if I need to go somewhere? he said. Ride your bike, Jo told him. They had rented one just for him, and he had not used it. Too much construction, he claimed. Not true, Jo said. You're just old and tired.

When the day came, Valpy said the scouts were making boats for launching on the lake the shape of Mexico. "We don't have any sails, wood, tools, or nails, but Captain Reynoso said he would help us with design." Penelope told him to go with the scouts. She would tell him about the bird museum later.

The road out to Señor Garza's hacienda in the Quinta María de los Desamparados was a stony and featureless thirty kilometers. Mr. Flatley said she would be reminded of the Holy Land, but as she'd never been there, she told him she would not. They rolled down the windows, and the air was dry and fragrant with a scent she didn't recognize, though it reminded her of Christmas. At times the spacing of the shrubs on the hillsides was so even, it put her in mind of a polka-dot print. Every person they passed along the road stopped walking and watched Jo's Buick go by as if a car hadn't passed in days. The few other cars they passed honked, and Jo happily tooted back. She loved driving, but when she was with Edward, he always took the wheel.

Some kilometers out of town, they saw a school sign with the motto "Molding to the future." "Hmmm," Jo said. "I'm not sure about that." Jo was the age Penelope's mother would have been. They drove in affectionate, companionable silence.

"Edward's working with the oils again," Jo said.

"But what about the San Esteban?" Penelope asked.

"He's left it for the moment, which is fine, except I was beginning to make progress on my own San Esteban, in oils."

"I don't understand."

"It's just his way. He doesn't let me work in the same material he's using. It's fine. I'll take the watercolors and do something else." Jo didn't seem particularly troubled, but a few minutes later she said, "I'm glad you proposed this trip. I needed a bit of cheering up. Edward says all my pictures are born dead."

"He said that?"

"Actually he drew a caricature of one of my canvases in a tiny coffin. That's his way of saying that."

Penelope was horrified.

"Oh, sometimes he draws what he knows he shouldn't say. Never mind, it doesn't matter. He doesn't like me to show my paintings to visitors, but I wondered if you'd like to come by."

Penelope said she would. Jo said Edward had started talking about leaving Fonseca early. "He thinks warmer weather will help his cold, but really he just doesn't like it here."

"He's a realist in a magical place," Penelope said.

"Do you think it's magical?"

Penelope pointed to the flock of starlings that had been following them, swooping and soaring above the road since Mirando.

"Maybe you're right," Jo said.

Penelope told Jo more about the circumstances of their visit to Fonseca, the Doñas, the legacy, and finally, the arrival of the Delaney and his claim.

"Oh my goodness. What a mystery," Jo said. "You must write a story about it."

Penelope had some working titles in the back of her notebook—Decadence, At Sea, Detour, Moneymore—but she didn't want to share them.

"Do you believe him?" Jo asked. "The Delaney. Could he be telling the truth?"

"I have no idea."

"Are you a good judge of character?"

Penelope had not thought about it one way or another. She knew her dear Uncle Wilfred had judged no one, which seemed almost impossible. Jo turned the Buick into Señor Garza's drive and there were Mrs. Slater and Mrs. Clancy waiting in front of the house. Penelope's sense of the pleasant afternoon drifted away.

"How did they get here?" said Jo. There was no other car.

"Hello!" the two women called as Penelope and Jo came up the jasmine-lined walk. "Isn't this lovely," Violet said, touching the buttons at the neckline of her well-fitted green dress. "I'm so glad Mr. Azuela could drop us off on his way to the mine."

"But how will you get back?" Penelope asked.

Violet smiled. "Well, we knew that you two were coming."

Jo rushed to say of course she'd be happy to drive them back.

"Are you interested in birds?" Penelope asked.

Before either could answer, Señor Garza greeted them all warmly. He was feeling much better and was so glad they'd come. For now, the Museo de las Aves was housed in his sitting room, which held about a dozen dioramas. He asked them to turn right just inside the doorway—it was a one-way exhibit—and proceed counterclockwise around the room. Considering the size and simplicity of the surroundings, the dioramas were impressive, of much better quality than Penelope had expected. The specimens ranged from the common mourning dove, starling, and Canada goose, to the less common yellow-headed blackbird, northern harrier, and Mexican duck. Notes explained common behaviors, including nesting and mating habits, functions of the beak, unique abilities, and general points of evolution.

"I'm afraid the collection is focused at the moment on birds of the north," Señor Garza said. One day, he hoped, the museum would be dedicated to all the birds of Mexico, north and south, east and west, coastal and highland. "Here is my rarest specimen." It was a black-bellied whistling duck, missing one eye.

One day patrons would move through the one-directional museum—he liked order, felt it had a calming effect on crowds—ending at a final door through which they would emerge into a beautiful secret garden filled with raptors, butterflies, and pond turtles. A giant statue of the Mexican national bird, the golden eagle, would welcome visitors at the front of the museum. A friend of his was already working on a design.

Mrs. Clancy looked confused. "Live raptors? Won't they eat the turtles?"

"Ah. No. The shell is too hard. In nature, they would grab the turtle with their talons, fly high into the sky, and drop it onto rocks far below to shatter the shell, but my raptors will be tethered to their perches. The technique will not work."

Penelope wondered how many times a tethered bird might try.

Violet went back to the mourning dove. The taxidermy was well done, the feathers glossy, the eye bright. The bird looked alert, almost quizzical, in its diorama bed of low grasses and shrubs. "I thought their eyes were blue."

"A common mistake. At a distance and in motion, it is easy to think so. It is actually a circle of blue skin surrounding the brown eye. Males and females of the species are very similar, the female only slightly smaller and duller," he added unnecessarily. It was the one thing they all knew about birds.

No one had any further questions, so Señor Garza led them into the back garden such as it was now, pondless, but with dahlias, perennial in the climate, climbing pink geraniums, and the classic yellow plumeria that bloomed nine months of the year, its fragrance strongest at night. There were a few impressive organ pipe cacti, and a winter-flowering mimosa tree with silver leaves and masses of fluffy yellow flowers. Penelope wondered if landscape gardening shouldn't have been Señor Garza's sole passion. White wicker chairs were arranged around a table of refreshments: a tray of tequila, lime, salt, and Montezuma beer. They settled, and without servants, Señor Garza served them himself, difficult to do from the depth of the bucket chair but he managed. Jo broke the awkward silence.

"I did not know a starling could be trained to speak," she said. In the museum, the starling diorama had said this was possible. The bird shown was in its winter, white-flecked plumage.

"They are great vocal mimics," Señor Garza said, "sometimes resented in Fonseca for their abundance and aggressiveness, but they symbolize unity, the group stronger together. Mine had a vocabulary of over one hundred words."

"Is—" Jo started.

"Yes, that's my Gemma in the diorama."

Violet glanced around the garden. She was sitting on the very edge of the cheap wicker chair.

"Charming," she said. "How long have you been . . . collecting?"

Señor Garza looked at the sky. "Going on thirteen years. Since 1940. I know what you're thinking: that's a collection rate of a bird a year. Ornithology is onerous, and I am getting older."

"That is not what I was thinking," Violet said.

"Could you hire another ornithologist?" Penelope asked.

"I have thought of it, but I have a large family and whenever I save a little money, there is always someone else who needs it more. I'm not good at saving."

"This is a general issue in Fonseca," said Mrs. Clancy.

Violet agreed. "My driver recently came into a little extra money selling flowers for the Day of the Dead. Did he put it in the bank? No. He paid an uncle and a cousin to shave him and clean his shoes. You will get nowhere with your museum this way, Mr. Garza."

"Oh, I'm not confused about that," Señor Garza said. "But Providence may intervene. You never know."

There was a lull in the conversation and Señor Garza went inside for more refreshments. Mrs. Slater turned to Penelope. "How are you feeling?"

Word of her condition had spread. "Oh, just fine," she replied.

"And where is Valpy?" Mrs. Clancy asked.

"The scouts are working on boat designs with Señor Reynoso."

"That's right," Violet said. "Little Valpy. He's been away from home for so long. He must be missing his father. And am I right you also have a young daughter?"

"I do," Penelope said.

Violet nodded. "My goodness."

On the way back to Fonseca, Jo's Buick bumped along the dry road, the air warm, the mood tranquil after Violet and Rose had a second round of tequila from Señor Garza. The flock of starlings seemed to have grown in number, but they reminded Penelope of Gemma stuck on her perch. They passed the school sign, "Molding to the future." Rose roused herself. "Yes," she said. "That's it. That's right."

"I've heard good things about that school," Violet murmured.

"Funny thing, though," said Jo, who didn't have children but was older than the rest of the women in the car. "A mold is made by casting into a shape that already exists. The future doesn't exist, so it doesn't really make any sense, does it."

"I'm sure they were not thinking of it in the *artistic* way," Violet replied, but she was quiet all the rest of the way home.

## ·· *Chela* ··

"Did you make any friends on the bus?" Chela asked. She had Valpy up on his stool, grinding cloves, aniseed, and cinnamon.

"There was a boy with marbles," he said. "He asked me to play."

"On the bus? How?"

"We had a mechanical problem that took hours to fix, so we played at the rest stop. We had to play outside, though, because of the different waiting rooms. The marbles didn't roll very well in the parking lot, but he had a travel game set, too, so when we were back on the bus, we played checkers."

"But where did you sit?"

"In the middle of the bus."

"And that was all right?"

"Until San Antonio." Valpy started scratching his right palm.

"Does it itch?"

"Yes."

"Left palm, watch your wallet," she recited. "Right palm, money coming soon."

He studied both his palms. "I don't have a wallet. It is definitely my right palm."

"That's a good sign. What happened in San Antonio?"

Valpy shook his head. "Let's work on my Spanish."

"Bueno. Cat."

"*El gato.* Too easy."

"Okay. A new start."

"Yes, please."

"Yes and how do you say it?"

"A new start? I don't know."

"*Un nuevo comienzo.*"

## ·· Third Sunday of Advent ··

*Viva Zapata!*, the big Hollywood movie starring Marlon Brando, opened at El Palacio theater on Victoria Street that December. Everyone in Fonseca was excited because the film, though shot in California, was said to be authentic.

"How?" Valpy asked. Two weeks of scouting had given him an appreciation for the local landscape.

"The director studied historical photographs," Mr. Flatley said.

It was the third Sunday of Advent, and Chela was taking the day to prepare for the coming Posadas, so a group from Mirando headed out to the Hotel Arizpe in the late afternoon to eat before the film. Worried about the likelihood of sitting next to the Delaney in the dark theater, Penelope decided to wear a bit of the L'Heure Bleue. If Desmond had wanted to remind her of the evening moment just before the stars come out, it was a failure. But if he wanted to remind her of their life at Chestnut Lodge and everything waiting for her, there was power in the bottle, and that is what she was counting on.

The Hoppers met them at the restaurant. "Edward's already seen it," Jo said. "Twice, I think. Is that right, Ed?"

Edward coughed and made an unpleasant face.

"Did you like it?" Penelope asked.

"There are several absurdities."

"Oh, do give us an example," Jo said.

"Well, for one thing, on their wedding night Zapata begs his wife to teach him to read."

"I bet she was delighted," Jo said.

"It is wrong to portray Zapata as illiterate," said Mr. Flatley. "He came from a wealthy, land-owning family and would have had an education. Mr. Steinbeck is inaccurate there, I'm afraid."

Suddenly there was a thunderclap and the light in the restaurant darkened.

"It must be nice to have a wife who is also an artist," the Delaney said to Edward.

"An artist?" Edward smiled. "She has a pleasant little talent, but what would be better is to have a cook."

"It's true," Jo said. "I am not a cook and I don't care. I don't like cooking."

"I don't like cooking either," Penelope said. "Pasta is the only thing I can make, and I sometimes serve cans of beans for dinner."

Edward rolled his eyes. "Oh, thank you. I'm sure that will be Jo's next delicacy."

When they left the hotel, a breeze gathered itself into a proper wind and tossed the climbing geraniums on the lampposts. Bursts of choir practice from San Esteban could be heard in the lemon-scented air, the heavenly chords well suited to the evening's towering pink clouds. Mr. Azuela joined them, and then Mrs. Clancy and Mrs. Slater. As they passed Mirando, the front door opened and to everyone's surprise the Doñas emerged, black veils still in place from Mass. They walked arm in arm to El Palacio in the bird silence.

The theater was crowded. Once the Doñas were seated, very close, their little veiled heads angled up at the screen, the rest of the group scattered. Penelope was aware of the Delaney waiting near her. She directed Valpy into a row with three empty seats, and the Delaney took the seat beside her. They looked at each other as the lights dimmed.

"Are you wearing scent?" he asked.

"I am," she said.

The Doñas had not left Mirando for anything other than church for longer than anyone could remember, and the experience invigorated them. Afterward, back at the house, delighted to find Chela who had returned to bake, they ordered champagne margaritas and the tres leches they smelled baking.

"That is for Tuesday, Doñas," Chela said. "Our night of Las Posadas."

"You can make another. Tonight we are celebrating *Viva Zapata!*"

"Are we," Chela scoffed, but went to the kitchen.

Mr. Tuttle said he had found the scenery convincing.

"Did you?" said Doña Elena, turning to him and scowling. "I could tell it was not Mexico."

"I liked the brother," Penelope said. "I think he should have played Zapata."

"Anthony Quinn is of Irish Mexican descent," Doña Anita said proudly.

"But Marlon Brando is the bigger star," said Doña Elena.

"Star or not his taped eyelids looked ridiculous." This from the Delaney.

"I don't know why they had all those lines about America being so wonderful," Doña Anita said. "The Americans interfered repeatedly, changing sides when it suited them."

Doña Elena stared at her. "I didn't know you felt so strongly about it."

"Of course I do!" Anita cried. "The Niños Héroes break my heart."

Mr. Flatley seized his opportunity. "Ah! The young cadets who defended the Castillo de Chapultepec in Mexico City during the war. When defeat was all but certain, they wrapped themselves in the Mexican flag and jumped to their deaths rather than be captured by the invading Yanquis."

"Is that true?" Valpy asked.

"It is taught in all the schools. Mexican children learn early it is better to die with honor than suffer humiliation from their northern neighbor."

"Mr. Delaney," Elena said, changing the subject. "I've been meaning to ask you. It's curious. I've written to friends in New York, and no one has a particular memory of you or your family's company."

"I hope they have a general memory?" the Delaney answered in his charming way.

"No," Elena said.

Mr. Azuela stepped forward. "Won't your family be expecting you home?"

The Delaney smiled and turned to the Doñas. "You are my family," he said graciously.

"We didn't know you a month ago," Elena said.

Anita waved her hands to clear the air. "It's no matter! You're here now, and we are all delighted."

Whether it was the fresh air or the joy of the third Sunday of Advent, Elena was in unusually high spirits, and after confronting the Delaney, she sought no further quarry. She told Chela to turn on the front lights and show any caller—even the mariachis—into the drawing room.

"Salud, salud, salud," raved Jasper.

The Delaney put a hand across his chest. "Thank you, Doñas. I am deeply grateful for your hospitality. I should also say, my family is mostly in New Jersey."

"New Jersey?"

Chela returned with the tres leches, reminding the Doñas in her darkest tone that Las Posadas began in two days. Nevertheless, she also brought out a platter of Irish shortbread and an enormous capirotada. No one was brave enough to ask why Chela had made a Lenten treat in December. Everyone there just felt fortunate to eat it.

The Hoppers had come to Mirando for the first time, and Edward had left Jo on a settee by herself to look at the art around the room. Penelope was about to go to her, when suddenly Mrs. Slater appeared. "Mrs. Fitzgerald, so good to see you again. How are you?"

Penelope put a hand to her belly. "I'm fine. I told you, I feel very well. Really."

"Oh, I'm glad to hear it." Violet took a meaningful sip of her drink. "But I was sorry to hear about your husband. My husband was briefly headed down the wrong path, you know."

Penelope, reviewing her interactions with Violet in Fonseca, couldn't figure out how she knew.

"Oh, I know it's hard." Violet sipped again. "You must be so worried about Valpy."

The cruelty of other mothers was not new to Penelope. A neighbor in Hampstead—not Mathilda, though she suspected her of harboring doubts as well—once knocked because she thought Tina had been in the pram in the back garden too long. "If you're going to leave her out there," she said, "at least give her a proper blanket." She'd brought one over and held it up. Her mother might have known how to handle these women always on the lookout for weakness, but not Penelope. Of all the reasons Penelope wished she had not had to navigate motherhood without her own mother, this one was the most acute.

Violet pressed further. "You look so surprised! Milo said Valpy was asking about the word *borracho*." She laughed. "The scouts love to help Valpy with his Spanish."

"That's not true!" Penelope said. "He learned that word from Chela."

Violet's eyebrows shot up.

Penelope recovered herself and looked around the drawing room, where at least half the people had clearly had too much to drink. "Valpy is observant. He's aware of these evenings. He often helps Chela prepare the ingredients, in fact."

"Of course, of course. I understand. It's just that he said his father . . . Oh, never mind. I'm sure he didn't know what he was saying. What do you think of the scouts?" Violet asked.

"They're wonderful. Why? I love everything about them."

"Don't tell me you came all this way so your son could run around with the sons of Mexican laborers?"

"They have been wonderful friends to Valpy. All of them," Penelope said.

"Well, of course. They know why Valpy's here. Of course they want to be his friend. Most of the Mexican scouts attend St. Ignatius on Calle Juan Aldama." She paused, waiting for Penelope to react. When she didn't, Violet said, "Not St. Ignatius on Calle Abbott."

"You'll have to tell me the difference," Penelope said.

Violet whispered, "Juan Aldama is *Roman* Catholic. Very poor. At any rate, the scouts are fine for Milo while he's little, but, you know." She made a face to suggest her Milo would soon be moving on to greater things. Years from now Penelope would have a name for people like Violet Slater, but in this moment in the drawing room of Mirando, all she could think of was "monster."

Eventually she made it to Jo, still alone on the settee. Penelope asked after Edward.

"The Doñas gave him permission to wander the halls, apparently. He says the art is all dark portraits and bland landscapes and he doesn't know how anyone can live around it."

Penelope was about to say there was a maritime scene on the second floor she thought had some merit, when Jo pulled her theater bill from her bag and showed her the back of it. Edward had sketched a couple, clearly himself and Jo, sitting at a nice table and sharing a large can of beans, Jo—and only Jo—tipped sideways with flatulence. "He made it during the film. Usually he leaves them around for me to find, but he handed me this one."

"Oh dear. I shouldn't have said anything."

Jo tucked it into her purse. "It's funny."

"You save them?"

Jo was embarrassed or had revealed more than she meant to, and like an animal covering its tracks, she lashed out. "Of course I do. They're very good. You would too."

"Of course," Penelope said quickly. But she couldn't imagine Desmond ever saying anything as cruel as Edward's sketches. She caught the Delaney's eye across the room. He was in conversation with Mr. Flatley and looked pained. When the Delaney noticed her, he raised his glass, and she smiled and did the same.

"Could I still come to see your work?" Penelope asked Jo.

Jo had a smile in which one side of her mouth went up and the other side went down. It was sweet and resigned all at once. "That would be lovely," she said.

The party continued until midnight, when Doña Elena rose from her chair to put on one of her favorite pieces of music, the cantilena from Villa-Lobos's Bachianas Brasileiras No. 5. Because it was beautiful and haunting and she played it over and over again, it subdued the party in stages. Elena stood swaying to the music, her hand curled to her chest with a drink. When Bidu Sayão hit the last note, the high A natural, holding it for what seemed an impossibly long time, Elena was still until it was done, then she replaced the needle and played it again. Her face was composed, a faraway look in her eye. Doña Anita was very still and, upon closer examination, actually asleep. When Doña Elena started the cantilena for the fourth time, half the guests left. The sixth time, Mr. Flatley and the Tuttles excused themselves. By the seventh time, Chela and Mr. Azuela, who was quite borracho in his bright blue suit, began to clean up.

The music played on and on and could be heard, it was later said, throughout Fonseca, as far as the Santo Cristo del Ojo de Agua. After Villa-Lobos, the Doña played Verdi, Puccini, some Mozart, but only the andantes and adagios, and finally back to the cantilena and its gorgeous last note. There was a scent of cigarettes in the air, though the Doñas, it was widely known, hadn't smoked in years.

The next morning, from her bed, Elena ordered the tile floors resealed. This was because whenever her hangover was particularly bad, she found solace in making extra work for others, Chela said.

Fonseca tile was unique in that it was left unglazed and unpainted, but had to be sealed to prevent water damage. Opinions varied, but most agreed the sealants lasted no more than fifteen years, and the ground floor of Mirando had last been sealed in 1920, during the revolution.

Jesús began by testing each tile by throwing water on it. If the drops were absorbed instead of beading on the surface, he marked the spot with blue tape. Valpy was delighted to help, all parts of the job appealing to him. By noon, blue crosses dotted the floor, thick as a graveyard.

## *Painting*

While the drawing room of Mirando was filling with blue crosses, Penelope went to Guajardo House to visit Jo. Edward was out. "Finally, a bike ride," Jo said. "I hope he doesn't crash. It's been a while."

On an easel in the middle of the room was another view of San Esteban, about the same size as Edward's, but in oil. The dome of the church was more prominent than in Edward's watercolor and less harsh, the colors softer, more integrated with the surrounding landscape. Penelope knew immediately that it was very good.

"I like yours better," Penelope said.

"You haven't seen it yet!" Jo cried.

"I can tell." But she walked over and studied it quietly for a few minutes. "It's good, Jo. There's a kindness in it and an understanding of Fonseca."

Jo was pleased but embarrassed and busied herself making tea. She invited Penelope to sit and showed her a few more pieces, studies mainly, of a chair, a cornice, a potted palm. Penelope liked them all.

"I know you draw," Jo said. "Who are your favorite artists?"

Penelope said her favorite painting was *Death of the Virgin* by Mantegna, which she once got to see twice in one year when it visited London from the Prado. She said she also loved Velázquez's *The Waterseller of Seville*, at Apsley House, and took the children there whenever she could. "I point to the man in the shadows between young and old and tell them that's their father."

Jo laughed, a face-lifted, full-throated laugh that was infectious. "Ed's hard to live with too. I used to let it bother me, but I made up my mind. Tell me about your husband. I don't even know his name! How is that possible?"

"I married an Irish soldier. Desmond."

"How old were you?"

"Twenty-six. It was ten years ago."

"So you had some time before the children."

Penelope nodded, then said, "Well, the war."

"I wanted children," Jo said, "but it was too late. I don't think Eddie would have been good with them anyway." She brought the tea over. "Do you think love is wanting the same thing? Two people wanting the same thing? That's what Ed says."

"Because you are both painters?"

Jo smiled. "Because we both want him to paint well." She refolded her napkin in her lap. "But is that it, or is it rooting for each other to succeed?"

Penelope didn't know what to say. Desmond did support her, but she didn't want to say so and hurt Jo.

Jo smiled. "For a long time money was a constant problem, and now it's not. I can make some sacrifices for that. Plus, he needs me. I keep all the books!"

"But how long can you go on like that?" Penelope asked.

"What do you mean? We've been married twenty-eight years. I made up my mind." She sipped her tea. "How are things at Mirando?"

"I don't know," Penelope said. "Sometimes I think Doña Elena must have written to us on a drunken whim. Other times I think Doña Anita is about to give Valpy the legacy. The worst is when I begin to worry there might be no legacy at all."

Jo looked at Penelope's middle. "And you're carrying a sweet bundle of more expenses."

"Yes."

"Don't worry," Jo said. "Make something of this trip and you won't have to regret it, whatever happens."

Dear ——

I have discovered (to our surprise!) that the old ladies I met in Saltillo were indeed spinster heiresses. Apparently William Purcell married Helen O'Sullivan (British but born in Mexico City) in 1874. He died with no surviving descendants other than three unmarried daughters. In the neo-Gothic residence he built, his unmarried Purcell-O'Sullivan daughters lived on. So not quite as crazy (or invented!) a venture as we had always thought.

I find the whole notion fascinating. Do keep the questions coming if you wish.

The bus was one of the old Super Coaches or "Silversides." A few years later we might have been on the Highway Traveler or Scenic Cruiser, with picture windows, air shocks, and in the case of the latter, sky window viewing, all of which might have improved things. US Highway 35 comes down from San Antonio, crosses at Laredo, and goes through Monterrey to Saltillo. This is the route we took. The bus was segregated, as this was a decade before the 1964 Civil Rights Act. I do not recall PM discussing this with me, or preparing me for the realities of it, but then I was only six.

Best wishes,
Valpy

*· A Birthday ·*

Thursday, December 18, Valpy woke Penelope with a surprise. "Rollos de canela!" he cried. "I made them with Chela."

Penelope was a Sagittarius, which meant nothing to her. She'd been told it was a mutable sign and suggested adaptability, flexibility, that she was a born explorer. Fine. Perhaps. What was definitely true, however, was that her birthday was December 17 and she had very intentionally not mentioned it to anyone.

"This is very nice, Valpy. What a surprise. Is Chela in the hall?"

"No, it is her day off. I carried it up myself."

He'd wrapped a gift in purple tissue paper, though "wrapped" suggested a degree of tidiness the package did not possess. What Valpy solemnly handed her was a crinkly purple ball held together with the blue tape she recognized from the tile-sealing project. She opened it slowly. She couldn't fathom how he'd bought her a present. There was no spending money for him on this trip, though she didn't think he harbored any bitterness about it because he knew she had very little herself.

His concentration on her progress was fierce, and though she could tell he wanted her fingers to move faster, he did not try to help the way Tina would have. Finally, she reached the last layer, and she still didn't have a good guess, meaning she would be surprised for the second time that morning.

The gift was round and flat with a weight that belied its size. A pendant? She pulled off the last bit of purple paper, and there in her hand was a large silver coin, half the size of her palm.

"It's a Caballito peso," Valpy whispered.

"It's beautiful."

"It's the most beautiful coin ever made."

"Where did you find it?"

"Caballito means little horse."

Penelope looked more closely at the coin. One side showed the Mexican coat of arms, which demanded admiration for its sheer narrative complexity. Not just an eagle like the United States coat of arms to which it bore a resemblance, but an eagle holding a writhing snake in its beak, while standing on a cactus growing out of a rock in the middle of a lake. Challenges upon challenges! On the other side was a woman riding a horse, her hands lifted high with a torch in one and a branch in the other. Behind her a sun crested the horizon, its rays beaming heavenward, while the horse pranced and bowed its head.

"Is that a laurel or an olive branch?" Penelope asked.

His frustration with her growing, Valpy took the coin back.

"The Caballito peso was made to commemorate the Mexican Revolution and they were only made for four years. See this?" He pointed at the first ray on the left-hand side of the horse, which was a bit shorter than its counterpart on the right. "In 1911 the design changed. They evened out the rays."

She did not understand.

"This is a 1910, short ray, Caballito peso, Mama." He said the words slowly, his voice full of awe.

"Where did you get it? Did you find it in the garden?"

"Yes." He handed the coin back to her.

"Does Jesús know?"

"Yes."

"I shall cherish it, Valpy. Thank you."

He looked steadily at her.

"It's very rare, Mama. Mr. Flatley said it is in excellent condition. The luster, strike, and friction are all superior, he said."

"It's beautiful, Valps."

"You don't understand! It's worth a lot of money! Don't you believe me?"

"Oh, Valpy. Why do you think we need money?"

"Chela says everyone who comes to see the Doñas needs money."

## *Love?*

At this point in Fonseca, Valpy had seen through the enterprise, at least to some extent, and the Delaney was a significant distraction. It seemed like a good time to question whether she should continue at Mirando or immediately book passage home. Her Uncle Dillwyn had always said, Nothing is impossible. Uncle Wilfred's motto had been, Get on with it. Uncle Ronnie liked to say, Do the most difficult thing. She loved them all, but these were very high standards. All of them, right back to her bishop grandfathers, distrusted wealth. But bishops and professors were given housing.

"I wrote to Desmond about you," Penelope said. She was walking with the Delaney around the lake the shape of Mexico.

"I'm flattered."

"Don't be. I told him this is all a very strange fairy tale."

"What did he say?"

"He said I am the wandering heroine and you are the tricky stranger in town."

"I think of myself as charming, not tricky."

"Well, they're not opposites. You could be both."

She had no earthly reason to do it, but before she could stop herself, she reached up and touched his hair. It was uncanny the way it consistently fell in such a fetching way across his forehead. This might have been minor enough, but when his smile faded and he looked at her directly, she felt again that recognition that stirred in her something she was trying not to remember, something she would not call love. But wanting someone's attention was the beginning of attraction. She did remember that.

She pulled her hand away and looked at the water. "I read somewhere that if a box turtle is removed from its home territory, it will spend the rest of its life trying to get home again."

"Fortunately, we are not box turtles," the Delaney said.

Penelope's father always wanted everyone to be happy, though he could be quite gloomy himself. How she would have liked to consult her mother. She might have been able to tell Penelope where the wiggle room was for a bit of happiness. How it might be possible to live as her uncles recommended and still raise a family and make progress toward something for yourself. What would her mother think of the mother Penelope had become? Would she praise her? Penelope had dreamed recently that she was playing between the rose hedges at Balcombe, and she was so happy to hear her mother's voice calling. Come in, come in, she called. There is so much I want to tell you.

The next day a letter from Uncle Ronnie arrived. Penelope had written to him of her conversation with Father Bedoya. She called him a shape-shifter, explaining that if one day he felt the Doñas were looking favorably upon art, he spoke of stained glass windows, their uplifting effect, and how he dreamed of replacing the mundane ones in the nave of his church. If literacy was the interest of the day, he revealed hopes for a parish library. His repertoire was boundless; there was no interest of the Doñas he could not bend to the need of San Ignacio on Calle Abbott. "You should take my place at Mirando," she wrote. "You would do so well." Her uncle Ronnie had always had just the right sort of personality to charm a room.

In his reply her uncle told her a little flattery is not inherently bad, particularly with the elderly. "In other words, compliment the Doñas, which I imagine you have not done." He knew this would be hard for her, in keeping with his advice to always do the most difficult thing. He also told her not to worry so much. If the legacy didn't work out, he would help as he could. And he said his vote was for the stained glass windows. "I remember how moved you were the first time you saw the Burne-Jones Last Judgment at Birmingham."

She left Valpy in the garden with Jesús and headed out for a long walk alone. She intended to explore new areas, but before long she was in the Alameda Zaragoza, staring at the lake the shape of Mexico. The water was unnaturally blue, and the white cement bank was the worse for wear since a large flock of geese had arrived. Undeterred by the excrement, a number of boys were launching little boats. Some kind of contest seemed to be under way, and she was sorry to see one towheaded boy, his enthusiasm getting the best of him, place a foot wrong and slip in.

The bank manager in her mind had been quiet recently, but

now he arrived for the grim interview she'd been avoiding. "Valpy is just coming into his memories, the first he will have for the rest of his life. Don't you agree, Mrs. Fitzgerald?"

"I do wish sometimes he were less observant."

"What will he make of this trip?"

"It's a concern," she agreed.

"Legacies are dangerous," the bank manager warned.

"But why?"

"They create an unnatural community of people. Every Pretender is thinking of the one thing he most wants if he could afford it."

"Or she."

"Yes, of course. Are you expecting to prevail, Mrs. Fitzgerald?"

"Not at all, but I'd hate to see Mrs. Slater ruled out so soon."

"Really? That is surprising. We'd have thought your support of her case as likely as . . . as . . ."

It was the usual trouble when bank managers attempted metaphor.

"But surely there is a tradition of like-minded communities bound by common financial cause?" she said. "One thinks of libraries, small museums, publishers?"

"Yes, and what do they all have in common? They are needy and full of internal strife. Good and evil, and the state of play between them, are clearer in a small community."

"Take then that fellow who is head of the Crafts Section at the National Museum. He is committed to the service of beautiful objects and the public that stands so much in need of them. That is a worthy cause."

"Notoriously tricky territory. Beauty is in the eye of the beholder, etc., etc."

"Well, Reynoso's scouts are a model of good behavior." She thought fondly of Reynoso and his boys. She wanted them to have all the equipment in the world: compasses, flying saucers, birdies, and balls. Whatever they desired.

"Plans that benefit children make us uncomfortable. We do not remember being a child."

"Then take Mrs. Clancy! The legacy should go to her. She is very strong and ambitious."

"Her idea may be a front for something else. Possibly nefarious."

Penelope was shocked, but pressed on. "What about Mr. Azuela? He is full of pity for the donkeys."

"Donkeys?"

"The decommissioned ones who are being frightfully misused."

"We are not concerned with animal welfare. Let's move on, Mrs. Fitzgerald. Do you know why your husband drinks?"

"Of course. What I don't know is why he doesn't stop."

"Mrs. Fitzgerald, is the Mexico trip only for the legacy?"

She didn't answer.

"Mrs. Fitzgerald, is it true that your friends and family don't know all the reasons you came to Mexico?"

She knew this line of questioning would peter out if she ignored it.

"Is it true you couldn't bring both of your children? Or were you just trying to make things easier for yourself?"

There was no right answer here.

"Is it possible your reason was clouded by the hormones related to pregnancy? Could you be experiencing unusual mood fluctuations?"

"I never did with my first two pregnancies. I don't see why this one should be different."

"You are older. But Mrs. Fitzgerald, another possibility. Is it true you submitted a story to *The Observer*'s short story contest in 1951? And that watching Muriel Spark win that contest, altering completely the path of Muriel's writing life, not to mention her finances, you felt irrepressible envy?"

"She's abandoned her son with her parents in Edinburgh!"

"That's not the point, Mrs. Fitzgerald."

"That story came from her years in Africa. I will admit it occurred to me that I had no experiences that far from home."

"And then Doña Elena's letter arrived?"

"Yes."

"Presumably you know that the English writer Agatha Christie also ran away from home, also in the winter, also when she was thirty-six years old?"

"She had one child and did not bring her."

"Agatha returned after eleven days. What do you intend to do?"

"My husband helped me plan this trip," she said defensively.

"And the Delaney? Were you going to bring him up, or shall I?"

Penelope had hoped the interrogation wouldn't take this turn.

"At dinner he has begun to make comments specifically to see you smile, and you are guilty of the same."

"—"

"Mrs. Fitzgerald?"
"We have discussed love at first sight," she said quietly.
"Oh?"
"I don't believe in it."
"And what did he say?"

## *Chela*

Valpy was on his stool grinding allspice and anise, and Chela was telling him about the Christmas desserts but also the rosca de reyes for Epiphany. She said she could not allow him in the kitchen when she made it because no one could see the secret present baked inside. Pax was lying stretched on the floor, belly toward the stove, purring loudly.

"What kind of secret?"

"Something special, and if you find it, then you are king for the day."

"What does that mean?"

"You tell everyone else what to do."

"What if Doña Elena finds it?"

"She has never found it," Chela said firmly.

Valpy finished his work with the mortar and pestle. "The bus driver said he was king of the bus."

Chela stopped working. "In San Antonio."

"He took a man to the sheriff's office."

"Is that where he wanted to go?"

"Oh no. I'm sure the man didn't want to go there. We couldn't play any more games after that."

"Valpy—"

"I know. Don't go back that way." He hopped off his stool and said quietly, "But when are we going back?"

Chela stopped her stirring and gave him the kind of hug she didn't think he got enough of. "Un abrazo de mamá, Valpy," she said, squeezing hard. "Me entiendes?"

He was only six, but he thought he did understand.

## ·· *Las Posadas* ··

Because Fonseca was above the coastal plain, it had plenty of humidity and rain. It was hot during the spring, mild the rest of the year, and during the cooler winter months, especially December, it was known for occasional snow and frosts at night.

Las Posadas ran for nine days beginning on December 16, one day for each month of the holy pregnancy, ending on Christmas Eve. On Friday, December 19, when the knock came at Mirando's door for the first time in years, Chela turned the procession away. A calm young Mary on a healthy donkey was unperturbed by the change, but Milo Slater, playing Joseph, looked panicked. In the crowd behind him, which included the mayor, treasurer, town clerk, and other dignitaries, his mother cried, "But it is a frosty night and they have come so far!"

Chela looked at Milo. "You have come from Doña Sotos two streets away. Come back tomorrow."

"Okay," he said.

"That was not the schedule," said Violet Slater.

"Let them come in, Chela!" cried Doña Anita. "This was our night."

"That was before the champagne margaritas, Doña," Chela said.

"Las Posadas have never been to a fourth house," another voice from outside cried. There were shouts and cheers and hoofbeats.

"And yet you can see how it would work," said Chela. She started to close the door. "Return to Doña Sotos," she said quietly to Milo. "I know she has extra pay de queso and arroz con leche. If she says she doesn't, she is lying. See you tomorrow."

The boy turned his donkey.

The Church of San Esteban's nativity play was the following evening, Saturday, December 20, and several from Mirando attended. Milo again played Joseph, though paired with a different Mary, and Genaro did a superb job as the magi bearing gold. However, his height and natural stage presence made gold seem like the superior gift. "It sends the wrong message," Penelope whispered. "They are supposed to be equal."

"Agreed," said the Delaney.

"I wanted to be frankincense," said Valpy.

The infant Jesús was played by a local baby boy, no more than three months old, whose mother hovered in the vestry, anxious to see the young Mary support his head correctly. And indeed, there were a few precipitous moments, but all ended well. No one forgot their lines and the nuns were pleased. They served refreshments afterward in the parish hall and gave a figure for the nacimiento to all the players. Even Valpy got one, a little donkey.

After congratulating Jesús on the performances of several of his nephews who had played sheep, Penelope, the Delaney, and Valpy prepared to walk back to Mirando. They were met at the church door by Violet and Milo. Penelope complimented Violet on Milo's performance, and years from now she will wonder why. What kindness did she possibly owe Violet Slater? But that's the problem with kindness. It cannot be turned on and off by those who feel it. "Oh, Valpy," Violet said. "Were you in the play? I didn't see you."

Milo looked at her. "You know he was not," he said, and Penelope saw in his earnest expression that, at least for now, the boy was kind.

Valpy admitted it was true.

"Oh, I'm sorry," she said, sounding not sorry in the least. "I must be confused. I thought the figurines were just for the children who participated."

"The nuns said it would be unfair to the children who have been here all year," Valpy said.

"Do you know I sometimes forget you are only visiting!" Violet said brightly. "You must be so homesick."

The Delaney stepped in. "The Doñas have taken such a liking to him," he said. "That certainly helps, doesn't it?"

The expression on Violet's face revealed this was her greatest concern, but she needn't have worried. A baffled Valpy looked up at Penelope. "They have?" he asked. "I almost never see them."

Violet turned her smile back to Penelope. "Well, I know Milo will miss Valpy when you go. All those fun scout activities. The other day he asked if Valpy might spend a night at our house. Would you like to?"

Valpy nodded, and Violet said she would propose a date soon. "But we mustn't keep you. After all, it's almost five o'clock."

THAT NIGHT IN THE DRAWING ROOM, Penelope decided to approach Doña Elena alone. She had in mind her uncle Ronnie's advice and thought she would say something about the back garden, especially the roses, which, she'd learned from Jesús, were originally planted by Elena when she was a young woman. But the Doña spoke first.

"Are you a believer, Mrs. Fitzgerald?" the Doña asked, already on her third gimlet. "Father Bedoya said you are not Catholic."

"My husband is Catholic. I was raised Anglican, but one of my uncles was an Anglo-Catholic, and another has become Roman Catholic."

"You converted when you were married?"

"I did not."

The Doña was surprised. "But here you send Valpy to the nuns?"

"I agreed to raise the children Catholic as part of my marriage vows."

"Why?"

"I've always thought the most important thing is to be a believer. The distinction was more important to my husband."

"Then why not convert to Catholicism yourself? For the sake of the family?"

For a moment Penelope wondered if the Doña would make awarding the legacy contingent on her conversion.

"My mother was Anglican, and for her sake I remain where I am."

Elena accepted this. "I went to London during the revolution here. For a time I attended St. Thomas More Church on Frognal in Hampstead."

"That is where I was married." It seemed a remarkable coincidence. "That is my husband's church."

Unfortunately, the Doña had moved on. "Do you save money, Mrs. Fitzgerald?"

Penelope was unprepared for the pivot from faith to money and hesitated.

"Mrs. Clancy was telling me something the other day about the native attitude toward insurance. She says the European community saves and plans for the future. The native population apparently does not." Doña Elena rang the bell for Chela, and when she came in, the Doña asked her if she saved any money.

"For what, Doña?"

"For yourself. To live on when you can no longer work."

Chela smiled. "Oh no. Of course not. My cousins and nieces will take care of me then."

"But without money you will be a burden to them!"

"That is why I employ them now, whenever I can, whenever I have a little extra money."

"So they are saving?"

"No, I don't think so."

"This is madness," said the Doña.

"Venimos prestados," Chela said sweetly.

The Doña gave her a withering look, and Chela translated. "'Our lives are only lent to us.'"

Doña Elena shook her head. "What about Jesús? Does he save any money?"

"Jesús has fourteen nephews!"

"I had no idea," the Doña said. "No idea at all. This is terrible."

Chela left to bring in the cart, for it was five o'clock, and Penelope made a last-ditch effort to follow her uncle Ronnie's advice.

"Doña Elena, I've wanted to tell you how much I admire the garden at Mirando. It is beautiful."

Elena turned to the window and tipped her head, a contemplative look on her face. "My mother brought the dahlia tuber roots from Ireland. The dahlia is a cherished flower of Mexico, but I suppose mine are Irish."

"I'd love to see them in bloom."

"But they bloom in summer," the Doña said, causing both women to wonder about the length of Penelope's stay.

## *Fourth Sunday of Advent*

"He was found wandering in the street with no one to care for him!" Doña Elena said, her voice bright with drink. It was one of her difficult days, and she'd started even earlier than usual. Doña Anita and Mr. Azuela had joined her.

"I protest that characterization." Penelope turned to Valpy, who had come home early with Jesús. Chela had alerted her that there was a crisis brewing in the drawing room, and she'd come down from her room ahead of the visiting hour. "Were you lost?" she asked Valpy.

"No. I was headed straight from San Esteban to the Alameda Zaragoza to meet the scouts."

Penelope turned back to the Doña. "I have always known him to walk with purpose."

"And I have never known Jesús to lie," Doña Elena said.

"He said walking, Doña," Chela said. "Not wandering."

"Walking, wandering," Mr. Azuela said unhelpfully.

"Where were you?" Doña Elena asked.

"I was writing in my room," Penelope said. This was apparently an unsatisfactory answer, and everyone waited for her to say more. It was the last Sunday before Christmas, the day the mother of God is honored, her love and dedication exalted. At Mass the reading had been the Annunciation according to Luke, and in the homily the priest made much of "El sí de Maria," how they should all be inspired by "El sí de Maria" to find obedience and joy in their own journeys. "El sí de Maria" Penelope heard over and over again.

Valpy spoke first. "Pax was with me, Doña."

"Pax often walks with him," Penelope said. "He won't go as far as the Alameda Zaragoza, though, for that is the territory of Doña Lopez's cats."

"You sound like Chela," Doña Elena said, squinting suspiciously.

"I agree." Penelope was bewildered. But she was not surprised that her mothering would be questioned on this particular day. It seemed in keeping with the rules of Fonseca.

That evening, there were Palomas and champagne and trays of Chela's Christmas cookies. The Hoppers arrived, and after a drink or two, while Jo was talking to Señor Garza across the room, Edward approached Penelope.

"I have a proposal," he said. "I want to paint a double portrait of you and Jo as a surprise for her birthday in March. I know she would like it."

"Watercolor or oils?" Penelope asked.

"Watercolor," he said promptly. "Why?"

But Penelope next asked how it would be possible to keep a double portrait secret.

He dismissed the question. "I have painted Jo many times."

Penelope questioned his motives. She knew what a double portrait could do, and he was often comparing her to Jo since he'd learned more about why she'd come to Fonseca. Edward saw her as supporting Desmond's career, and he relished pointing out to Jo that she had never done anything so brave or dramatic as crossing an ocean to raise money for them in their desperate early years.

It had inspired a caricature. He'd given it to Penelope the last time he saw her: a rainbow with a pot of gold at the end, but the rainbow traversed a formidable mountain range, impossible terrain he represented with harsh strokes of the pen. She was a small figure in the foreground, disheveled, disorganized, yet somehow determined. Like all his sketches, there was truth in it, but if truth had both good and bad elements, he had a knack for locating just enough of the bad to hurt. She was squat and stooped. She'd put it in the back of her notebook. Jo was right; she planned to keep it.

She told Edward she would think about it.

Later she sat with Jo, who told her Edward was miserable. "He's annoyed at the town, sick of the changeable weather, unhappy with the landscape work he's doing. He has orange and ocher and cream quite well, but he is struggling with the blue, as you know. Still. We talked the other day about Pre-Raphaelite blues, but those are all in velvet and silk, he says, and he wants light, distance. I understand, I do, but he is just impossible."

Penelope didn't know what to say.

"At any rate," Jo said, finishing her champagne, "he has some new idea now that seems to interest him, and he's stopped talking about leaving early, so that's nice."

*Christmas*

The bells of Fonseca were baptized and confirmed in the faith just like the parishioners for whom they tolled. Peals of the large bells could be heard up to five kilometers away; the smallest could reach up to half a kilometer. The largest cathedrals, such as Our Lady of Guadalupe in Mexico City, might have as many as 16 bells. A large parish church, such as San Esteban, typically had around 8, while a small village church like the Santo Cristo del Ojo de Agua might have 6 or even only 4. With 4 bells only 24 different musical combinations were possible, whereas 6 bells made 720. To the mathematical, this was simply the factorial function at work, but to the devout it was a sign of God's bounty no less wonderful than Jesus feeding the multitudes.

On December 25, the sun rose at 7:28 a.m. and the bells of the thirty churches in the diocese of Fonseca began at once, the peals rising in waves from every direction. They seemed to gather and grow above the Zona Centro and to set the windows of Mirando singing in their frames. In many ways all the practice sessions were for naught because, such was the joyous cacophony, it was impossible to distinguish one set, one church, from another. Later some said the bells of San Esteban did the best in the lower ranges and the Santo Cristo del Ojo de Agua had the distinction, as always, of being the last to finish. All the bells rang for half an hour as the sun rose on a Fonseca sugared overnight by five centimeters of snow. At 8:00 a.m., when all the ovens opened, there were still flurries so light they didn't appear to be falling, just sparking the air.

Valpy had accepted with astonishing equanimity the idea that presents would not be opened on Christmas morning, but he still wanted to mark Christmas in his own way and had asked if he could sleep under the tree Christmas Eve. The idea came from a book they had at home, an edition of Clement Moore's *The Night Before Christmas* with charming illustrations, one of them showing a heap of pajama-clad children asleep under an enormous tree.

"Are you sure, Valpy?" Penelope asked. "You will be alone."

He was sure.

Penelope was prepared to say no, but to her surprise the Doñas thought it was a lovely idea. Chela frowned and said with all the cooking she had to do for the holiday dinner that night, she would not have time to make a proper bed for him on the floor. But she was not opposed to Christmas night, and so that is what he did.

Having outdone herself on Christmas Eve, Chela made Christmas dinner a simple meal of leftovers, and everyone retired for the evening relatively early. Penelope tucked Valpy in next to the tree, its lights casting the front hall in a sweet glow.

"Valpy," she said, kneeling beside him. "We are owed nothing in life. You know that, right?"

"But do we deserve nothing?" he asked.

"I didn't say that. That's not the same thing." She took a breath and started again. She wanted to demonstrate more command and control. She knew it would better alleviate his worry. "What I mean to say is that we are fine. You and I and Daddy and Tina. If we stick together, we will be fine. Families can endure a lot as long as they do it together."

"But we aren't together. Daddy and Tina are in London, and we are here."

"That's temporary."

He didn't look convinced, and she suggested they make lists. She had some paper with her.

"All right. But do you have matches?" Valpy asked.

"Yes."

And so Valpy wrote that he would like ten Flyin-Saucers, enough for all the scouts, a ride on an airplane, and a figurine of the Virgin Mary, because when the nuns had handed them out on the fourth Sunday of Advent, he didn't get one.

"Why?" Penelope asked.

"Because you are not Catholic."

"Oh, for heaven's sake. You have a Catholic father and great-uncle!"

"What did you put on your list?" he asked.

"To hear the muezzin. A trip to Russia. A rose garden."

"What is the first one?"

"The church bells here remind people to pray. In Islam, the muezzin sings. His voice carries a long distance."

"Like Captain Reynoso's."

"Yes."

Valpy looked at her, concerned. "Are we going to Russia next?"

"Oh my, no. Not yet anyway."

"I'm tired of traveling."

"You should never tire of traveling. Now go to sleep."

She stood and went up to bed herself.

The wind was up, and the house creaked and thumped. The rain sounded like waves breaking against the window. A cold draft came in under the door, circled her chaise, then the desk. Penelope lay with her eyes wide open, ears pricked, astonished by her racing pulse and annoyed with herself for being so silly. It was just a storm! But at the stroke of midnight, the wind seemed to strengthen and lash the house even harder. She thought she heard someone laugh in the hall. Finally she threw off her covers and went to check on Valpy.

She found him sitting up, hugging his knees, a number of the nacimiento figures around him. When he saw her on the stairs, he came running and threw his arms around her waist. It's true she was not a hugger. Something in her held back; she didn't know why. But she never forgot the strength of that hug.

"I'm so glad you came," he said.

"You are?"

"I thought this would be fun, but it isn't."

"It's this storm. A quiet night would have been different." But she saw there was more he wanted to say, and she waited.

"I keep thinking about the donkey from the market. Where do you think he is tonight? It's Christmas."

"It makes me sad, too, Valpy. I'm sorry we can't help that donkey, but I like to think there will be another animal someday we will help. Because we saw him. Does that makes sense?"

"Yes, but my stomach hurts."

"What did you have for dinner?"

"Pollo asado, but Chela was distracted and forgot the oregano."

"Do you want me to stay with you?" Penelope asked. "Or do you want to come upstairs?"

"Upstairs, please." He put the figures back in their proper places in the manger and started to fold the blankets from Chela, many more than he needed. "I think I saw a doña borracha."

"Which one?"

"Anita."

Penelope sighed. "Probably."

Suddenly there was movement in the corner of the hall, and Valpy said, "Is that the ghost?"

Penelope looked at him. "Have you seen a ghost?"

But it was the Delaney. "Not a ghost," he announced, holding up a blanket. "I was worried Valpy might be cold."

"Chela would never allow it," Penelope said, trying to avoid his eyes. "There are at least a dozen under the tree."

"I see that now."

There was a long silence, until Valpy said, "Thank you, though."

The Delaney tossed the blanket over his shoulder. "Well, it's back to bed then. Shall I walk you up?"

The three started up the stairs, and Penelope felt again the cold of the library.

"Valpy! Are you cold?" she cried.

"No, Mama. I'm fine. Are you?"

She didn't answer but took his hand and squeezed it. He loved it when she did this, and he squeezed firmly back.

At the top of the stairs, the Delaney said goodnight and turned right. Penelope and Valpy turned left. Pax, watching them from the hall, lifted one paw and gave it a delicate lick.

In their room Valpy still couldn't fall asleep.

"Close your eyes," Penelope said. "Try the Lord's Prayer."

"The Rosary might be better."

"Have the nuns given you beads?" It was her understanding this would not happen until he was ten.

"No, but Chela says they are not strictly necessary." His eyes were beginning to close. It took some time for his breath to slow into sleep, and Penelope stayed at his bedside, waiting and watching. Outside it was snowing lightly. She was still unsure about the birds on Sundays, but this snow silence, the same all over the world, she could hear.

Valpy opened his eyes. "Mama, at the Santo Cristo del Ojo de Agua there is a waterfall." He sounded troubled.

"Yes?"

"If it is a water eye, then does that make the waterfall tears? I asked the priest on the field trip, and he said no, they don't think of it that way. 'Why would such a beautiful symbol of faith be crying,' he said."

"Valpy. It is just like that. That makes it more beautiful."

He settled back on his pillow. "You know as a non-Catholic you can still request the seal of confession and receive a prayer, but not absolution."

She told him to go to sleep; it was almost half past two. She was not in the habit of crossing herself. It was not the tradition she was raised in. But sometimes, because of Desmond and now the children, she imagined her fingers touching those points—forehead, heart, shoulder to shoulder. There was comfort in it.

Dear ———

Yes, "PM" stands for Penelope Mary. I always use this in correspondence about her because "my mother" seems too impersonal and "mama" too personal.

The big Christmas dinner was on Christmas eve instead of Christmas day, but with mole (bitter chocolate and chilies) dressing the turkey. And the presents were on Epiphany when the Three Kings come. I remember the rosca de reyes which I was told had a secret present in it. I found it in my slice, but it turned out to be a dry bean.

My birthday was 30 January, and I do remember the piñata—the gardener pulling it up and down on the rope, and me trying to hit it with a stick so the sweets would fall out. In fact, they were not sweets, just bits of sugar cane.

I do hope this helps,  
Valpy

## *Love?*

Every day between Christmas and New Year, Penelope either wrote to Desmond or walked with the Delaney, or both, and the fact that she liked both activities equally seemed to her a not insignificant problem. She enjoyed working with Desmond on the journal long-distance, though in her letters she frequently reminded him of the effort she was put to in Fonseca.

"What is the plan," she wrote, "if I don't succeed? I don't think you understand how truly precarious our situation is. We are on a precipice." Every time he replied that she would succeed because she always did. He believed in her. And if for some reason she did not succeed, then they would sort it out when she was home.

IN THE ALAMEDA ZARAGOZA, she and the Delaney always sat on the same bench, their arms touching from a point just above the elbow to the shoulder. It took an ungodly amount of concentration for her not to lean into him. They sat like that for hours, talking, on the edge of the lake the shape of Mexico.

The Delaney acknowledged the difficulties of their situation and felt they should decide what to do, how to proceed or how not to proceed. But Penelope could not decide anything. "Decision is torment for anyone with an imagination," she said.

"Maybe matters of the heart are not decided. They just are. They just happen. Isn't that what the poets say? The mind need not play a role."

"You can't be serious."

"I am." He looked hurt. "I certainly didn't come here for the legacy and expect to fall in love."

"That makes two of us."

"So you admit it!"

"I believe we are each half-in-love," she clarified, "and that makes only one whole love and nothing can be done with that."

"I disagree."

She shook her head. "Besides, I have a baby coming."

"I know. Three children under seven. It won't be easy."

"Chela thinks it's a girl."

He took her hand. "Penelope. This is a love story. It's not convenient, I agree, but that is what has happened."

"It can't."

"Are you in love with your husband?"

She remembered being in love with him.

Desmond's letters remained roughly the same in length, but hers were growing shorter. Despite the writing she was doing, she found it hard to put into words all that was happening in Fonseca. When she tried it sounded fantastical, which she detested. She did not believe she was a good-enough writer to let magic creep in.

Desmond understood this.

"I know you are having many experiences," he wrote, "and they are accumulating in your mind. Whatever happens, I know you will make use of it all. Don't worry. I believe in the fullness of time I will see Fonseca as clearly as you and Valpy do now."

But he was mistaken there. She did not see Fonseca clearly at all.

Desmond mentioned they would need to run an errata, their first, in the February issue. "Maybe more of an apology. What do you think of an *errology*?" This was regarding the story "Jones Disposes" by Michael Voronetz from the December issue. "He's quite upset. Apparently we didn't run the whole story. I do remember cutting it down, but I must have failed to tell him."

She wondered how badly the cuts had been done. It was only a four-page story! She responded that he certainly shouldn't call it an *errology*.

Desmond wrote about his efforts with the advertisers. "After hours of intense negotiation, during which I used some of my best rhetorical, not to mention military, training, all but one agreed . . .

to stay at exactly the same rate. Only Black & White whisky agreed to an increase in exchange for the back cover."

Penelope hung her head. This meant more cases showing up at Chestnut Lodge and more long lunches for Desmond with the account executive.

"I hope the Tate won't mind," he continued, "but they did have a chance. It's possible the V & A will fill in. I'll try them. If not, I'm not sure we're going to make it to August."

For a moment Penelope wasn't sure if he was referring to the journal or their wedding anniversary. But it was the last paragraph that made her feel like crying.

"At the close of day, some people will drink and some will not and that is how it has been and always will be. I just have to figure out a way *to do it right*."

She couldn't bring herself to begin a reply. Instead she wrote to her mother-in-law, asking again for news of Tina. She drew a little black cat, sitting very upright, the way Pax did, tail neatly wrapped across his front paws.

Valpy had a letter for his friend George Wilson, which she included in a letter to his mother, apologizing for the front gate and saying she would see to it when she was home.

"WHAT IS THE PLAN?" Penelope asked the Delaney. They were on their bench. "Does one of us get the legacy? Or do we do without, your skills suddenly needed at your family's company, if it even exists. What is your relationship with them?"

"Not serene."

Penelope didn't blink. "Right. So were you thinking of moving to England?"

"No one is unfettered," he countered. He had been saying for days, "What are the chances?" as an argument for the destiny of their meeting.

To which Penelope countered, "I believe choice should play a role."

"Chance and choice are not opposites," he said, "if you have faith."

Penelope threw up her hands. "I arrived in Fonseca with a financial dilemma, and you are making me return with a moral one!"

"What are the chances?"

"How can I just choose?" she said. "How can I just choose an entirely different life?"

"Because that is what it means to live!"

"But I married an Irish soldier!" she cried.

The Delaney put his head in his hands. "So you've said."

"If I could make it so that he would never be unhappy again, I would. But I can't, so staying is the only choice I have."

"But how long can you go on like that?"

"We can go on like that for the rest of our lives, I think. Most people do." But her heart wavered, and she took his hand. Their meeting in Fonseca, whether fortunate or the opposite, was as inscrutable to her as the concourse of the stars.

"We are a missed connection, Ernest."

"Not missed. We are here now."

"It is the wrong time."

"Because you met the wrong person at the right time?"

"I think so."

"I don't care for your worldview."

They sat together in silence, Penelope still holding the Delaney's hand. In fact, she was having trouble letting it go. "Desmond is not the wrong person," she said finally. "He is kind and good. The situation is difficult, it is true. But how can he be punished for that?"

"He is not punished, as far as I can see. You are. And now I am too." He pulled his hand away.

MAYBE IF DESMOND didn't love poetry. Maybe if he didn't write so well. Maybe if they hadn't stayed up late many nights when they were younger talking about painting and music and architecture. Maybe if he hadn't known and loved her uncles as much as she did. Could there be comfort without continuity? She wasn't sure. She had simply entrusted too much of herself to him.

Maybe if he became unpleasant when he drank. If he got angry or loud instead of quiet and sad.

Maybe if he hadn't cried with happiness when Valpy was born. Maybe if he didn't hold Tina so gently and read stories aloud so well.

Maybe if she hadn't gone to that Oxford party. If they hadn't married during the war. If he hadn't been sent to Italy after North Africa.

Maybe if she didn't remember how he held her when he got back.

Maybe if she still had her mother. If her eyes didn't follow mothers and daughters with their babies everywhere she saw them. What would that feel like, to have your children and your mother?

Maybe if he didn't bring her daffodils every year the first day they arrived in Covent Garden. Maybe if he didn't love the trombone section's entry in the *Egmont* Overture as much as she did.

Maybe if she believed he could manage any amount of money.

Maybe if he didn't love bicycles and Beckett and political cartoons. Maybe if he cared about clothes. Maybe if he preferred Marylebone to Hampstead, the mountains to the sea, crystal over pottery. Maybe if he didn't understand why she loved to shell peas. Maybe if he complained about her cooking, or housekeeping. Maybe if he complained about anything.

Maybe if he were competitive. Maybe if he didn't believe she would one day write a great book. Maybe if he hated animals!

How many things would have to be different for her to change her life?


The Delaney said, "I dream of you." They were walking back from the park.

She didn't respond for two whole streets. "I have two kinds of dreams in Fonseca," she finally replied. "I dream of my mother, or I dream of crumpled banknotes that for some reason it is my responsibility to press."

"I dream of you," he said quietly, again.

"You do not."

"I do. Fully clothed, of course."

Her cheeks burned all the way back to Mirando.

LETTERS TO DESMOND and walks with the Delaney. Back and forth, back and forth.

"What are you doing?"

It was the bank manager again. She admitted she was beginning to lose track.

She did, however, have the clarity to refuse Edward's double portrait. When she told him, he shrugged it off as a momentary interest that had already passed, but the next time she visited Jo at their rooms at Guajardo House, she saw he'd begun a portrait of Jo, off-center, on a large canvas.

"I like this one," Jo said. "So far, at least. We'll see what happens, and I'm not sure about the composition." The painting was in its early stages, but he was clearly giving her a double chin and an unkind expression about the mouth. "What are you up to with all this space?"

"I'm going to paint a tree."

"A tree?"

"Yes. A jacaranda, I think."

"But jacarandas are blue. Not another blue, Ed, please."

"What do you think?" he asked Penelope.

"I would avoid another difficult blue," she said, and Edward laughed.

"The truth is," he said, turning to Jo, "I'd planned to surprise you on your birthday with a double portrait of you and your friend Mrs. Fitzgerald."

Jo looked stunned for just a moment, then she shook her head. "I don't think that's a good idea. You paint women unkindly."

Penelope tried to intervene with excuses about why she couldn't sit anyway, but Edward bellowed, "It's fine! It doesn't matter. I'm planning the jacaranda!"

Dear ——

I have been thinking about the whole question of the pony prize. It must have been Ma who got me to enter the contest and prompted me to write the story. But why? In Southwold we already had a mixed group of scruffy old ponies which were kept in a field on the marshes up by the gas holder. I went up before school on winter mornings to fill up the hay nets, and we children rode everywhere unsupervised and free. I also remember going to the little corner shop with a half crown to pay for the rent of the field. By this time my parents were already completely broke and struggling so why did we have the ponies anyway let alone accept a prize of another one! My parents weren't particularly horsey people. And most extraordinary, there was a choice between saving certificates and the pony and she chose the pony, which when it arrived was a completely unsuitable, highly strung, nervous animal. So one more mystery in my mother's life.

She was a very keen gardener though she never had a garden of her own until she moved in with us in Almeric Rd. This was a tall thin Victorian house with a small back yard which had been half concreted over and neglected. She threw herself into clearing it, transforming it by hand, breaking up the concrete with vinegar and hammer and chisel and building a small brick terrace at the back to catch the sun. It was soon a riot of color and climbers and gave her a great deal of happiness.

When she moved back to London to live with my sister, who is herself a keen gardener, she had the front of her ground floor flat and the side entrance where she grew the most magnificent roses which can be seen in the last portraits of her. She was also very interested in medicinal herbs and plants, now of course very usual but not then.

My diary of that time just records chocolate cake and small presents for our birthdays and I imagine that was always the case. Neither of us can remember any actual birthday parties.

With best wishes,<br>
Tina

## ·· A Question of Law ··

The argument began when Doña Elena asked Mr. Whishaw, the solicitor, to call the day after Christmas. As everyone in Fonseca knew everyone else's business, the drawing room at Mirando was full by four o'clock. Chela, asked to bring the cart early, did not do her best work. The Manhattans were weak, slightly warm, and without cherries.

The grandfather clock in the front hall chimed the hour, surprising everyone with its accuracy. Generally, it chimed unpredictably, no one having wound it regularly in years. Chela claimed to have forgotten how, and the Doñas never knew. With great internal effort the clock still roused itself occasionally, but the sounds preceding the bells were jangly and discomfiting. As the clock settled down, Garden Club, Hospital Wing, and Silver Guild all rushed in.

"What is the collective noun for a group of Pretenders," the Delaney said to Penelope.

She proposed a "flutter."

"You are thinking of butterflies," said Mr. Flatley, who had come up behind them.

"We are not," Penelope and the Delaney said at the same time.

A few minutes later Mr. Whishaw arrived, sweating through his suit.

"You are the right Mr. Whishaw?" asked Doña Elena. "I do wish I could tell you and your cousin apart."

He said that he was.

Doña Elena turned and addressed the room. "I've asked Mr. Whishaw here today to explain a few details of the law as it pertains to legacy gifts."

Mr. Whishaw pulled a fat stack of papers from his briefcase.

"Oh dear," said Doña Anita.

"Don't worry, Doña. The law can be long-winded, but I will boil it down." He turned to the room. "As you know, the Delaney mine was very profitable for many years. And after nationalization, the Doñas' subsequent investments have done very, very well."

The fluttering around the room increased.

Doña Elena closed her eyes. "No one knew that, Mr. Whishaw."

"It is what they have been saying at the supermercado," said Garden Club.

"How helpful. Let's skip over the details of private financial arrangements, Mr. Whishaw, and discuss the bequest."

Mr. Whishaw held up a hand. "Ah. Now, technically a 'bequest' is money given upon a person's death. I believe you are interested in an 'inter vivos' gift, money given when someone is still very much alive."

"Indeed," said Mr. Azuela.

"So that depends on the trust document. For example, I could say, 'I promise to give this money to you in five years.' That is what we call a naked promise. But a naked promise is meaningless unless it is transactional, so the law allows for a 'consideration,' something given to make the contract binding."

"This is confusing," said Doña Anita.

"I'm sorry, Doña. Let me explain. If you promise to sell me this chair, for example"—he put his hand on the back of Mrs. Clancy's chair—"the contract is for the chair; my promise to pay you is the consideration."

"What if the contract gives the legacy to a minor?" Mrs. Clancy asked.

"In the case of a minor, a trust would be created and the trustee would be bound by fiduciary duty to invest it wisely and only in the beneficiary's best interest."

"Are we allowed to set terms?" Doña Elena asked. "That is my specific interest."

"Yes, some, but you cannot make a stipulation that, for example, ties the money up beyond the lives of the people alive at the time of the gift."

Doña Anita frowned.

"You cannot say, for example, 'He shall have the money when spaceships fly to the moon.' You cannot make demands that are considered controlling from beyond the grave, you see? You also cannot give the money contingent upon someone changing himself. You cannot say"—he looked around the room and pointed to

Mr. Flatley—"he can have the money if he promises to stop reading books."

Doña Elena pointed to Hospital Wing. "What if we asked him to be more specific?"

"As a general rule—"

"Oh, I love a general rule," Mr. Flatley said.

"No one is surprised," said Doña Elena.

"If you gave him the money and he built something else, you would not be able to take the money back again," Mr. Whishaw finished.

Doña Anita looked alarmed. "But that's terrible! What if none of them does what they say they are going to do?"

Mrs. Clancy spoke up. "My husband began as an itinerant salesman and now has a dozen *aprendices* under his care! Of course we are accountable." She pointed at Penelope. "If you give it to her, what will she use it for? Have we ever heard?"

"If I may," Mr. Whishaw said. "The law regarding gifts to minors informs us here. It puts some restrictions on those keeping the money for others. But no doubt Mrs. Fitzgerald and her family would benefit to some degree. That is not strictly forbidden."

Everyone turned to Penelope. It was true. She'd been in Fonseca almost two months and had never spoken of her plan for the legacy, should it be given to Valpy.

"Mrs. Fitzgerald," said Doña Elena not unkindly, and around the room, the Pretenders regarded Penelope with jealousy. "What is your plan? What would you put the money into?"

"A literary magazine."

There was laughter. Disbelief spread through the room like rumor over a battlefield. Several people rubbed their foreheads, trying to remember the last time they'd seen one of those, or even just the last book they'd read.

"It's called *World Review*. I have issues in my room if anyone is interested." Though the issues she'd brought were a poor version of what she dreamed of making if money were not a concern. Every issue would have art, criticism, interviews, essays, stories, poetry. She dreamed of a removable broadside in the back printed with a poem like the rhyme sheets she'd loved as a child from the Poetry Bookshop. They would run annual contests, with good prize money and the promise of publication. Desmond would edit; he was a brilliant editor when he wasn't drinking. From their already extensive coverage of European art and literature, they would expand to the Americas. They'd published Salinger and had a story in from Mailer. Why not the great Latin American magical realists? Eventually they might become a small press, like Hogarth, but in Hampstead instead of snooty Bloomsbury.

Señor Reynoso was the first to speak. He said he would be proud to subscribe and would make sure the Universal Children's Center always had several copies available. "I've noticed," he said, "that children often understand a poem without it having to be explained to them."

"Yes," Penelope managed. "Yes, that's exactly right." She could have hugged him.

"I'm sorry, what did you say?" Mrs. Slater said. "Universal Children's Center? What is that?"

"Oh, it's a wonderful idea," Doña Anita said. "Señor Reynoso wants to build a center with everything children need: books, musical instruments, sporting equipment, tutors in every subject."

"When was this proposed? Why have we not heard about it?" Mrs. Clancy's displeasure was so pronounced, Violet Slater, friend and coconspirator, put a hand on her arm.

"We were not aware that you had to be informed of all developments," Doña Elena said.

The Delaney stood. "I think we can all agree that law and legacies aside, the Doñas' hospitality is to be celebrated." He lifted his glass. "To the Doñas."

Penelope caught his eye but did not lift her glass. She was beginning to think she didn't have the strength to participate in this contest any longer, a battle she clearly missed the start of and that would likely end long after she was gone, if it ever did. But what was the alternative? *World Review* was on the verge of bankruptcy.

She wrote to Desmond that night. "We will have to leave Chestnut Lodge. We might have to leave London. A different church I can accept, but a different home?"

Dear ——

I must say that I did not have a sense of her "waiting" when I was a child growing up. Apart from the fact that the thoughts and motivations of adults are an impenetrable mystery to all children, and resisting the temptation to read time backwards, my recollections are much more of PM being impatient to do new things rather than patiently waiting to fulfill a dream. The impulsive journey to Mexico is one such instance of course, but there were many other "means of escape"—often with me.

"Something lacking but not necessarily wished-for." Yes, this translation of "desideratus" sounds like a promising strand of thought. Certainly PM was an obsessive list-maker throughout her life, as I still am now. She always told me that if you get what you wish for, it never turns out to be as simple as you thought.

Regarding the excursion in Mexico City: We went on a warm day to the Aztec pyramid of Teotihuacan, which seemed (and is) enormous to me. We took a picnic in a straw basket and left it at the bottom of the steps for later. From the top we watched a little boy of about my age steal the basket. I would like to think I sympathized with him, but I doubt it. The fact is, the basket also held our dinner.

I hope this helps,
Valpy

## *Holy Innocents*

Penelope told everyone she was writing a piece about Mexican art for an upcoming issue of *World Review* and needed to go to Mexico City. She could work from sources at the library, but she preferred to see the images themselves. She asked Jo if she wanted to drive and come with them, and Jo did, but she shook her head, then impersonated Edward.

"'I can ride my bicycle for an afternoon but not three whole days!'"

So Penelope bought bus tickets for her and Valpy and told the Doña about her plans on the Feast of the Holy Innocents. The day was cold, and Penelope came into the drawing room wearing the blue serape. Doña Elena's eyes immediately narrowed.

"Ah, there it is. You've been hiding it away in your room." She looked down and smoothed her lap with her palms. "Do you know our custom on this day?"

Penelope did not.

"It is a tradition on Holy Innocents to borrow something from a friend or family member, a playful sharing, as children do."

Having witnessed a fair amount of rivalry between children, Penelope was not sure she agreed with this description.

"I would like to borrow your serape," Doña Elena said.

Penelope was headed south, where she presumed it would be warmer, and so she readily agreed.

BEFORE THEY LEFT, Penelope needed to talk to Jesús about Valpy. She found him on the back terrace by the still-blooming rose garden. The chicken coop was toward the house, by the kitchen, and the birds pecked around, scattering when Pax appeared, though he had no interest in them. The winter mimosa was still blooming, and the jacaranda was beginning to bud. Someone had planted evening primrose along a border. It was all lovely and Penelope would have spent much more time in the Mirando garden if Jesús weren't so industrious. His work made her feel indolent in the sun with her notebook.

"If this is about the fourth Sunday of Advent," he began, "I did not intend to cause trouble. I should have come in through the kitchen instead of the front hall, and then Doña Elena would not have known about Valpy being lost."

"He was not lost."

"He was alone on Calle Juan Aldama."

Jesús was a steady worker, tall, religious. His clothes were worn from work but never dirty. She wondered if he had a wife who did this for him. Only his glasses were smudged, perpetually. He was building something, a frame of some kind, working with a saw and a drill, but he stopped when she approached. "It is the Caballito peso I need to talk about. Is it valuable?"

"It is rare."

"I understand. But Valpy—"

"It is very special."

"Is it worth anything?"

"It commemorates the one hundredth anniversary of Miguel Hidalgo's Grito de Dolores, which began the war of independence from Spain."

She saw she would have to be very specific. She stepped closer to the gardener and looked him directly in the eye, a move she had seen Chela employ.

"Is it worth a lot of money?"

Finally he was defeated. "Not on the scale Valpy thinks. I believe he misunderstood."

Penelope returned to a more comfortable personal space. "He is a little boy with no experience of money. You gave him the wrong impression."

"Mr. Flatley did not help."

"He rarely does."

Jesús took off his work gloves. "The day we found the Caballito, I didn't understand your financial problems."

"What do you understand about them now?"

"Valpy says you live in a house with many cardboard boxes and very little furniture. He misses his friend next door. He says this friend's mother often feeds him dinner."

"I've lost the Caballito, Jesús. It was in my pocket, and it must have fallen out somewhere."

Jesús took off his glasses and tried to clean them with the inside lining of a pair of gardening gloves. "That's a shame, Mrs. Fitzgerald. He will take it hard. He thinks you haven't returned home because you don't have the money."

"That's not true."

"I am only telling you what Valpy thinks."

"But the Caballito would not help us get home anyway. As you said."

"The Caballito peso is a gift of another kind. However, it is true that sometimes things long buried should stay buried." Jesús replaced his glasses, now grimier than before.

Penelope looked about the garden. The camellias were blooming profusely, their scent heavenly. "Why does everything grow so well here?" Penelope asked.

"The elevation," Jesús said.

THE BUS RIDE to Mexico City was nine hours but blessedly uneventful. After leaving their bag at the small hotel she'd found, they went immediately to see the Rivera and Siqueiros murals at the New University. She was surprised not to like them as much as she'd expected—she found them confusing and unsatisfactory—but the ideas behind Mexican muralism resonated with her. It was what she'd always loved about the Arts and Crafts movement, public art for the people, the distinction between the fine and useful arts minimized if not erased.

They visited the library of the original University of Mexico, founded by Charles I of Spain, now a museum guarded by a small man clad in a brown suit, holding an enormous silver key. They had to bang on the door for entry, and when he emerged, he smiled and showed them the doorbell at the side. He told them he was the guardia not a guía and held up his key. But then he directed them to walk back and forth twice to appreciate the illusionistic ceiling painting in the first room, pointed out a table of ebony (from India) and rosewood (from Brazil), and said the books were still used by students and the public, though there weren't many still on the shelves. He proudly showed them the white slips where books had been removed and taken to the library of the New University.

In the village of Metepec they saw a square full of women and children making clay toys like the ones they'd seen in the mercado. In San Miguel de Allende, a merchant tried to sell them something from a recent historical excavation that had turned up ancient clay mermaids. A mystery, as San Miguel de Allende was more than three hundred miles from the sea. She couldn't wait to tell the Tuttles.

The last day they went to see the temples at Teotihuacan, where they took a guided tour. When the guide began to describe the Aztec priest dancing in the skin of the young sacrificial victim, Valpy reached for her hand and Penelope whispered that sometimes great art and great violence were connected. Afterward, Valpy wanted to climb the Sun Pyramid because he remembered Mr. Azuela had said the mining pits were as deep as it was high. They left their lunch basket at the bottom of the long stone staircase and started up the 248 steps. When they made it to the top, they turned just in time to see a young Mexican boy racing off with their basket. Valpy was dismayed. "Mama!"

From the top of the pyramid, they had a long view of the boy's run. He crossed two streets, spoke briefly to a shopkeeper, tied his shoe, and kept going as fast as he could, around a corner and toward the avenue.

"Well, maybe he needs it more than we do. He's trying to grow up, just like you." Though Penelope had splurged on the elotes, tamales, and fruit in that basket—buying enough, she hoped, for their lunch and dinner—and was sorry to see it all disappear.

THEY RETURNED ON the first of the year, and the next day Chela fell ill. Her cough and congestion lasted only two days, but when it cleared, her sense of taste disappeared. In the morning she made chorizo y queso scones and enjoyed one fresh out of the oven, a January breeze coming through her open window. Two hours later she was making the dinner tortillas when she tasted one and thought she'd forgotten the salt. But there was her dark-blue ceramic salt box open on the counter, showing the impression of her pinches. She tested another one. The texture was perfect. She rolled it around her mouth, then she swallowed and screamed.

She'd lost her sense of taste once before, years ago, and the condition had lasted a week. She'd had to go home to her mother's house to recuperate, and so she immediately began preparations to do so again.

What was surprising was that no one else could taste the tortillas either. "How can this be?" said Doña Elena. "I have not been sick."

The residents of Mirando, all but Doña Anita, who had retired to her room again, had gathered on the brick terrace in the back garden. The scream brought most of them; Valpy had been with Chela. In fact, it was Valpy who told her to turn off the stove. Her sense of smell was gone, too, and she hadn't noticed her sauces were burning.

Mr. Flatley nibbled a tortilla. He said he could detect a hint of corn.

Chela dismissed him. "No, you can't." She was packing her knives. "If the ingredients do not work for me, they do not work for anyone."

"How can that be?"

"I cannot explain cooking to you now, Mr. Flatley."

"Can you smell or taste anything at all?" Penelope asked.

"A little gray."

"Ash?" someone said.

"No. Just the sense of gray. I must catch the four thirty bus from the Anáhuac Station," Chela said. "Esperanza will be here in the morning. As for tonight, I suggest you all eat out at the Hotel Arizpe. I told Don Pedro to expect the lot of you."

Jesús arrived with the car, and Chela bid them goodbye. She kissed Doña Elena, told Pax to be good, and hugged Valpy. Then she bundled herself into the front seat of the car with Jesús and was gone.

The rest of them were left standing in a semicircle. "Would you look at that," said the Delaney, pointing down. Before them the last bit of unmelted snow on the bricks appeared in a patch the shape of Mexico. As the group stared, Pax sauntered between Valpy's legs and seated himself squarely in the middle of the country, his long tail swishing over, and thus erasing, the Baja peninsula.

But Penelope was still watching the dust rise from Chela's exit. The ability to retreat to a mother's house to literally recover your senses seemed like the most magical thing she'd seen yet.

Dear ——

I remember the serape, though I honestly don't know what happened to it. I do know that she would always insist on any trip or holiday on bringing back some local object that had caught her eye even at great inconvenience. There were some incredibly heavy quilted Turkish bedspreads that smelt awful. Also Spanish pottery and metal Russian icon pictures.

As far as I remember the serape was mostly red with some yellow stripes and other colors. It was coarsely woven and you could see the vertical threads through the weaving. I suppose it must have been packed away when we left London. I agree it's a mystery about "the wrong colors." Wrong in what sense? She obviously thought I knew why they were wrong. You are right she loved strong vibrant colors and many of the rooms she lived in were painted olive or a rich forest green combined with a dusky blue.

I don't recall my mother ever talking about her trip to Mexico in later life, even though Valpy went several times for academic purposes and with his family.

Did she like cats? I would say she observed cats and understood them and was happy to have them around but she was not sentimental or openly affectionate with them.

Best wishes,<br>Tina

# JANUARY

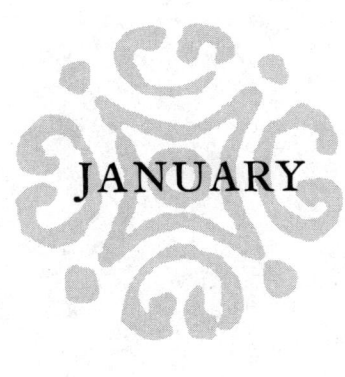

*· At Sea ·*

Chela was away for a week, and Mirando wobbled.

Monday, January 5, Esperanza let Valpy sweep the front hall. When she was pulled away for a kitchen emergency, however, she forgot to tell him to stop before sunset. And so Valpy, diligent in all that he did, kept sweeping, every corner, every stair, as the sun went down, a bad omen as it invited misfortune through the front door.

Tuesday, January 6, the Christmas decorations were not taken down. If they were not taken down on Epiphany, then they had to stay up until Candlemas. The poinsettias, already dark as blood with wilt, began to die.

Esperanza had made the rosca de reyes and served it with lunch. The party was small, only the Tuttles, the Delaney, and Doña Anita were there, in addition to Penelope and Valpy. Everyone was surprised when Valpy bit into the dry bean, not because he'd found the surprise, but because the surprise was a bean.

"That is not a proper rosca de reyes!" Doña Anita cried. Esperanza was called in to explain. "We always have a bean at our house," she said, with a lift of her chin. "No one told me it should be something else."

The Delaney turned to Valpy, who was still holding the bean in his palm. "Well, you are king of the day, even with a bean. Congratulations!"

No one felt festive.

"Mrs. Fitzgerald," Doña Anita said. "Why has my sister-in-law been wearing that lovely blue serape of yours?"

When Penelope explained, Anita was alarmed. "She borrowed it on the Feast of the Holy Innocents? But you will never get it back!"

"What do you mean? She said it was a tradition of the day to borrow something from a friend."

"It is a common trick."

"I am king of the day," Valpy said. "Can I make her return it?"

No one at the table thought this was a good idea, except Anita. "Yes!" she said. "Oh, yes! You must try. It is a holiday custom, after all, and she brought in a Christmas tree for you. Just don't go in if she is listening to the cantilena."

So later that afternoon Penelope and Valpy waited outside the drawing room until the cantilena finished. It was an hour before the visitors arrived. Doña Anita had gone upstairs, and Doña Elena was alone in the drawing room. They heard her move to the Victrola and lift the needle, though she did so heavily, scratching the record. "Mierda," she said.

"Mierda, mierda," repeated Jasper.

"Shut up," snapped the Doña, sounding unlike herself. Penelope's ears pricked the way they did when Desmond came home late.

Valpy looked to Penelope.

"Do you know what that means?" she asked.

He nodded. "Some of the sea scouts say it sometimes."

"She loves her records."

"I know," he agreed.

But as Penelope began to open the door, she saw Elena stumble. She steadied herself on the back of a chair, then made her way from the Victrola to the hearth using the furniture in her path, hand to hand, to support herself.

Penelope pulled the door closed. "Valpy, this is not be a good time."

"But I only have this one day to ask, and I will be upstairs later."

"Nevertheless." She moved him into the hall. "I'm sorry."

"Don't you want the serape back? I thought you liked it very much."

"I do."

"I don't understand. If Chela were here, she would know what to do."

"That is true." Penelope wished it weren't true, but it seemed better to be honest about it than to deceive both of them.

Wednesday, January 7, the drawing room learned of Violet Slater's boldest move yet. She had approached Doña Anita while no one was looking and convinced her to allow Mirando to be shown.

"Shown?" Doña Elena asked. "What do you mean *shown?*"

"She said it would just be small groups of the most interested people, historians and architects and art collectors, I think. And not too often, just once a week or so. Actually she suggested Thursdays."

"Isn't that Chela's day off?" Doña Elena said.

"We can change the day if refreshments are needed."

"Oh, well," said Doña Elena. "I'm sure Violet means well."

Nonsense, thought Penelope.

"Her husband's engineering firm has been doing wonderful work at the mine," Elena said.

"Doña, if I could have a word." Mr. Azuela had just arrived to give his daily report. "If you mean the Slater plan for deep shafts, I must disagree. It promises safer ventilation, but the model hasn't been tested."

"Dear Mr. Azuela. We all know that if it were up to you, the donkeys would still be pulling the arrastras." She ended the discussion and called for the cart.

Thursday, January 8, Valpy asked if the Caballito had been officially graded. Penelope told him not yet and then desperately resumed her search for it. She'd read that if you lose something, you should try hard to picture the last place you had it, but that was the blue room with Valpy and she'd looked everywhere. But she couldn't see it clearly. She remembered there was something special about the rays, but could not recall what exactly. She confided in the Delaney.

"Isn't it just a coin?" he asked.

"Yes, but it's historical and Valpy believes it is a treasure."

Together they searched the path around the lake the shape of

Mexico, the Church of San Esteban, the Hotel Arizpe, and Guajardo House. She even sent a message to Señor Garza.

"It is just like me to lose the most important gift he's ever given me. What if he never recovers?."

And Friday, January 9, the scouts had an accident. Their boat designs complete, Señor Reynoso acquired some scrap wood and tools and boat assembly began. No one saw exactly what happened, but when Milo screamed, Genaro was holding the saw. The wound was minor—it needed only a few stitches—but the incident allowed Violet Slater and Rose Clancy to start asking questions. Wasn't it time for the sea scouts to have a safer headquarters? And be organized by a proper leader? A whisper plot about Reynoso began to grow.

Violet hired Mr. Flatley to tutor Milo in history and French while he recovered.

Wriggling her way into the life of the villa like a worm, Penelope thought.

Finally, Saturday, January 10, Chela returned, all her senses restored. Everyone felt better and the grandfather clock in the hall chimed the hours, though incorrectly.

When she heard about Milo's accident, Chela scoffed. "Mr. Flatley speaks French?" she said. "Ridiculous."

## ·· *Ordinary Time* ··

Ordinary Time, symbolized by the color green, came after Epiphany. In Fonseca, these were peaceful, wintry days. Penelope spent many hours writing in her quiet room. The article for *World Review* was coming along, and she was beginning to wonder if she might also be able to finish the short story too. She went out only on Thursdays to escape Violet Slater showing Mirando. They all did, except Esperanza, who came to attend to anything Violet might need.

One of these Thursdays, Penelope went to the Hotel Arizpe for tea and saw Jo sitting alone. Usually gregarious and full of energy, she looked deflated, the only cheerful thing about her the red bead necklace she often wore. She invited Penelope to sit, and they ordered a fresh pot of tea and a plate of galletas María, both agreeing that Chela's were better.

Edward had the watercolors again.

Penelope stared. "Oh no."

"While he had the oils, I started a watercolor of the theater, El Palacio on Victoria Street, but sometimes when I start something, he gets interested in it and then he'll take the idea or do a version. So he has the watercolors back, and I've got the oils. It's fine. I'm hoping to finish my San Esteban now."

"You must," Penelope said.

"Are you working on anything?" Jo asked. "I still think you should write about Mirando."

Penelope said she was.

"That's wonderful. And Desmond won't complain and make you switch to nonfiction. How lucky."

Penelope believed it was a mistake to try to understand another person's marriage, but she couldn't help herself. "I don't think it's fair, Jo."

"Remember," she said. "I made up my mind."

Jo said she would get the bill, and while she was away from the table, Penelope took out a piece of paper. Her sketches had the comfort of labeled things, though she didn't label them. The strong, simple lines announced themselves: tea cup, laundry basket, potted plant. They were the very opposite of Edward's.

She drew a paintbrush for Jo.

SATURDAY EVENING there were strong martinis, and Doña Elena had so many she broke her glass, fell forward, and cut her breast. The next day she went to the garden to recuperate, a piece of muslin-wrapped ice on her chest, and ordered Jesús to build a rabbit hutch.

"What is this I'm hearing about a sea scout accident?" she said. A few of the other houseguests had joined her on the back terrace. "Mrs. Slater said her son was wounded by one of them?"

The Delaney, who was assisting Jesús with the hutch, looked up. "The boy exaggerates, Doña."

"Most children do," said Mr. Flatley.

"It was a minor incident," the Delaney insisted. "Milo had three stitches. He will be fine."

"Nevertheless," the Doña said. "This sea scout business has become serious."

"All children want their projects taken seriously, Doña," the Delaney said, and Penelope caught her breath, for it was one of her dearest beliefs.

The cantilena played from the window, where Elena had asked Chela to set the Victrola so the music could be heard outside.

"In the evening, a dreamy, pretty cloud . . ." Mr. Flatley began to translate.

Elena held up her hand. "Stop, please. If I don't know what it is about, it can be about anything." She closed her eyes. The cantilena finished, and Doña Elena, ice melting on her chest, fell asleep.

Unfortunately, Violet Slater moved fast. The next evening Mrs. Clancy told the drawing room that the sea scouts would be getting a building, their first real headquarters. Mr. Slater was converting an equipment shed near the lake in the Alameda Zaragoza, and he would also serve as captain until someone suitable could be found.

"But Señor Reynoso is suitable," Penelope said.

"We've told Reynoso he's no longer needed," Mrs. Clancy said. "Frankly, I think we are very lucky something worse didn't happen sooner."

"Who told him?"

"Mrs. Slater. She was glad to do it. She spoke for all the mothers."

"She did not! She did not speak for me!"

"That's not true. Mrs. Slater told him how close Valpy and Milo have become and how upset Valpy was about Milo's wound."

"He wasn't."

"Regardless, it was a blow for Señor Reynoso, but it's for the best."

"Blows are never for the best," Penelope said. "Where is he now?"

"Milo?"

"No, Señor Reynoso! Where does he live?"

"On the Viejo Camino, but his house was emptied this morning."

"Emptied?"

"He left and took only a suitcase."

Mrs. Clancy didn't know where he was going, and so Penelope went straight to the kitchen, to Chela, who told her it was too late. Doña Lopez had seen Reynoso waiting at the Estación del Norte, a one-way bus ticket in his hand.

"I thought Doña Lopez was blind," Penelope said. "How could she know he had a one-way ticket?"

"You do not need the power of sight to hear the weeping of a man's heart."

"When was this?"

"About an hour ago."

"When does the bus leave?"

"How would I know? I have never been to points north of Fonseca."

Jesús agreed to drive Penelope to the station, and when they pulled in, a number of buses were boarding. The lot was full of passengers, bags, children, and animals. Penelope walked up and down between the buses as best she could in the crowd. Someone asked if she needed help Someone else asked where her umbrella was. "It is going to rain," he said in English.

She kept walking, searching the crowd, scanning the passenger windows as best she could. Then, at the far end of the lot, a bus began to pull out, and she saw Reynoso's profile, halfway back. She waved her arms and called his name, but he was staring at his lap. The bus turned left onto the Avenida Presidente Cárdenas, then disappeared, Señor Reynoso aboard, his head bowed.

"What bus was that?" Penelope asked the stationmaster.

"The six fourteen to Piedras Negras."

"Is that near any water? Maybe a lake or a river?"

"Oh no, señora. It is desert, as dry a landscape as humans can inhabit and survive."

"That's terrible," she said.

"It's not for everyone," the stationmaster agreed.

The rain started and the streetlamps flickered on. Why wouldn't Reynoso head east, back to the water he loved? Why would he go to the dry and rocky north? The blow must have been terrible.

Penelope decided to walk back to Mirando; she didn't care that it was raining. She followed the Avenida Presidente Cárdenas to Calle Miguel Hidalgo, where a group of young men, drunk, did not make room for her on the sidewalk and she had to step into the street, turning her ankle. She passed a mariachi group with another broken donkey. She opened her purse, took out the largest bill she had, and gave it to the man holding the harness. He immediately took off his sombrero and insisted she have a ride. He indicated with his hands that she was not too big, it would be fine! His donkey was strong! She waved him off, repeating no gracias, no gracias, until she got away.

Almost to Mirando, she saw the Delaney sitting on a bench in the square. When he saw her, he rushed to her with his umbrella.

"It's too late. I'm already wet," she said.

"Where have you been?"

"The bus station."

The Delaney looked stricken. "Were you going to leave?"

"No. Señor Reynoso left."

He moved the umbrella to shield her entirely from the rain, leaving himself half in it. "I know. I'm so sorry. It's awful."

"How did you know?"

"Genaro was here. He came to see Doña Elena while you were gone."

"Genaro? Why?"

"He said it was his fault. He said he should have been more careful."

"It was not his fault!"

"I know. He thought the Doña could help keep Reynoso, but of course she'd already talked to Violet Slater." There were tears in his eyes.

"It was not his fault," Penelope said again, wiping her own eyes. They stood in defeated silence. Then the Delaney said, "Sit with me?"

"I'm soaking," she said.

"So you said."

"Your umbrella isn't doing any good."

"What are we talking about?"

Penelope regretted that her hair was hanging in wet streaks on either side of her head. She knew there was a drip at the end of her nose, and the baby was kicking. She didn't know what he saw in her, but she saw in him a person of determination, not fortunate, perhaps, but not also daunted.

"I still haven't found the Caballito."

He nodded.

"Ernest, I don't think I would have lost it if I hadn't been distracted," she said. "By you."

Suddenly a flock of starlings whirled up and out of the tree above them, the rain seemed to lighten, and Ernest leaned over and kissed her.

"Ernest," she said. "What are we going to do?"

He smoothed her hair. He said that right now they were going to go back to Mirando. They came in the front door to the music of Los Panchos, "Mar y cielo" playing in the drawing room. "Que nunca, nunca, nunca el mar lo alcanzará," the tenors sang. The sea never, never, never, reaches the sky.

Ernest didn't remember it.

"It was playing in the launderette," she said. "I told you I have a good memory."

THAT EVENING THERE WERE MANHATTANS, a favorite of Mr. Azuela's. Later, people would say he must have stopped somewhere before Mirando, that he arrived already unsteady on his feet, but no one knew for sure. He seemed pale and sweaty, and after two cocktails from the pitcher, he began pouring whiskey directly into his glass. By the time the day visitors began to leave, he was very drunk. Chela told him to go splash water on his face and clean up. Use the bathroom on the second floor, she said. He left the drawing room, and when he didn't return in a few minutes, everyone assumed he had gone home.

Chela announced dinner, and as everyone was crossing the hall on the way to the dining room, they heard a shout. Mr. Azuela, the arms of his jacket pushed up to the elbows, was at the top of the stairs. He held up a book, his index finger keeping his place. "Aquí!" he cried. "Aquí!" and rushed down the freshly swept stairs.

Later someone said they heard him say "Slater" as he descended. Others heard "soldier." Whatever it was, on the third stair from the bottom, his feet went out from under him, he fell backward, and his head came down on the edge of the sixth step with a sickening thud. He sat up immediately, but then flopped backward, sliding down the final few steps, one arm moving as if swimming, blood pooling from the back of his head and one ear.

Mrs. Tuttle screamed. Doña Anita threw up.

"A human being can survive the loss of up to a quarter of the total amount of blood—"

"Not now, Mr. Flatley!" Doña Elena cried, but it was the Delaney who actually pushed him out of the room.

Penelope lost her voice completely. She stood there swallowing and blinking, feeling that whatever mechanism it was that drove speech up and out of a body was utterly broken within her. Fonseca had done it. On the other hand, it surprised her that she did not feel more frightened. She had no rush of adrenaline, no rising panic. She said no prayer, though was sorry to realize she owed a debt of gratitude to Violet Slater. Milo had invited Valpy for an overnight and Penelope had let him go, despite her misgivings about Violet. The fiesta de pijamas had saved Valpy from a terrible memory.

Only Chela kept her head and called all her contacts for help, but by the time the chiefs of police, fire, and park services arrived, it was too late.

"Why park services?" Mr. Flatley asked. It was much later, everyone back in the drawing room, dinner abandoned. Chela was having a whiskey and didn't answer.

"We didn't even know his first name," Mr. Flatley said.

"Genaro," Chela said.

Penelope stared. "Was he related—?"

"Yes, of course. It's a family name."

The book he'd been holding was a history of Fonseca. Impossible, though, to know which page he'd wanted to show them.

The next day the bells of San Esteban tolled three times three, the protocol for a man who was deceased; women received two times three. Then the church tolled one stroke for each year of the deceased's life. As no one at Mirando knew how old Mr. Azuela had been, they listened and counted, a solemn wait through forty-two bells.

## ·· *Chela* ··

When Penelope finally went to consult Chela about the lost Caballito, Valpy was already there. He was sitting on his kitchen stool and he'd been crying. "You always tell me anything you carry about with you in your pocket you are bound to lose sooner or later."

Penelope looked at Chela. "How did you know? I've told no one."

Chela closed her eyes. "Doña Lopez saw you walking on Calle Juan Aldama, staring at the ground."

"But how did she know what I was looking for?"

"She sneezed in the middle of the street."

It was the final defeat of the nonsensical answer. Penelope turned back to Valpy. "I have always found the things I've lost, or that you've lost, or that you've given me that I've lost"—because this had happened before and she'd promised it never would again. She took a deep breath. "Valpy, I am very sorry."

"We always lose the things we like most!" he cried and ran from the kitchen.

Penelope felt as if she'd been punched.

"I pity you," Chela said, turning to her stove.

Suddenly exhausted, Penelope sat on Valpy's stool. "I think you 'have pity for' someone in English. It sounds better."

Chela considered a moment, then shook her head. "No, I don't think so." She wiped her hands on a towel, reached into her apron pocket, and pulled out the Caballito.

Penelope jumped up. "Chela! Where did you find it? But why didn't you say something? Valpy will be so pleased."

"Will he? You have told him it's true value?"

Penelope stared at the coin in her palm.

"You have a choice, I think. You can tell him the Caballito is found and that it is not the fortune he believes it is. Or you can let him believe and let it remain lost."

The peso was eagle-side up, the writhing snake in its beak no more caught than Penelope felt.

"To be honest, I feel a little lost." She returned to Valpy's stool.

"I pity you," Chela said again, and Penelope thanked her.

## ·· Another Birthday ··

Monday, January 26 was Tina's birthday. Tina had been born at half past seven in the morning, and Penelope woke on the minute. Thinking of her little daughter, turning three so far away, she lay on the chaise, unable to move. Tina would have loved eight o'clock in Fonseca, the rattling of the windows, which came right on time.

Valpy got up and dressed quickly. Penelope told him she wasn't feeling very well, so he went down alone for breakfast with Chela. He didn't mention Tina's birthday, and she thought it best not to remind him.

That morning Penelope went to the English-language bookshop on Victoria Street to see if she could find something to take home to Tina. She had not been able to convince Jenna from Ealing to carry *World Review*, but they had a friendly relationship because of all the letter paper Penelope had purchased during her stay. She came through the door to see Violet Slater browsing in the nonfiction section.

There was no one else in the store but the two of them and Violet's husband, Steve. Violet turned. "Hello, how are you?"

"I don't answer that question."

Violet smiled and turned back to the shelves.

"Um, Mrs. Slater and I were just discussing whether I should shelve the Bibles in nonfiction or poetry," Jenna said.

"You're buying a Bible?" Penelope said.

Violet laughed. "I want to read the Psalms. Father Bedoya suggested them."

"Why?"

"You sound so surprised! Comfort, I suppose, after what happened to poor Mr. Azuela. Reminders of the brevity of human life, eternity of God, et cetera."

"I thought you'd be more interested in the punishment of your enemies."

"What?" Violet said.

Penelope had Steve Slater's attention now too. "You took the scouts away from Señor Reynoso. The children loved him, but you had to get rid of him because the Universal Children's Center is an unassailably good idea." She thought she should probably stop and gather her thoughts, but she couldn't. "You are indelicate, inconsiderate, unfeeling, vain, and arrogant. You are a ruinous bully!" Shocked by her own bravery, Penelope took a step backward.

Violet was unapologetic. "Oh my. You are unhinged. You know everyone is saying your husband has left you?"

"If I'm here and he's in England, haven't I done the leaving?"

"So it's true, you are separated?"

"No."

"But how could you leave a child for so long? And you're having—" Violet looked at Penelope's belly, and her eyelids went red. She swallowed hard, suddenly unable to finish her sentence. The expression on her face was one of pure despair. Penelope remembered what Doña Elena had told her, but said nothing. She did not believe she could make her voice sound sympathetic.

"Listen," Steve Slater said. "Violet said you are here because you need money." He began to pull his wallet out of his trouser pocket, giving Violet an excuse to cover the emotion that had engulfed her.

"Don't be stupid, Steve. What are you going to do? Give her a couple of thousand pounds? That's not enough to help anyone."

Penelope never would have taken the money, but she didn't agree. That was the difference between people who had money and those who didn't; they didn't understand how much difference even a little extra made.

When Jo came to Mirando to tell Penelope they were leaving Fonseca, they'd already packed up their rooms. They were going to go farther south, to Guanajuato. Edward thought it would be better for his health and his work. He was still trying to get the right blue.

"You can't go," Penelope said. She wanted to say, "Don't go. Stay. Finish your painting." But with what authority? So she said, "I thought we might go see Señor Garza again." She wanted much more time to talk to Jo of art and husbands.

Jo smiled at her. "I would have liked that."

The wind was up, clouds moving in, and Penelope and Valpy helped them load a few last things into the car. Jo and Edward walked to the curb where the Buick was parked. They paused to argue, of course, then switched positions. Edward walked to the passenger door, and Jo got into the driver's seat. It seemed he was going to let her drive after all. Jo looked back at Penelope over her shoulder, pleased with the victory. As the car pulled away from the curb, Jo stuck her left hand out the window and waved, and kept waving, until she had to turn the corner at the end of the street.

The Hoppers returned to Fonseca in 1955, and Edward would exhibit work from the 1943 and 1955 trips, but never anything from the winter of 1952–1953. Years later Penelope would see Edward's final double portrait, *The Comedians*, and the catastrophe of the pair's clasped hands—Jo's left, Edward's right. The hands made no physical, geometrical, or even anatomical sense. They were a knot, a swirl, a storm. And Jo's lips were bright red, pursed like a clown's, while his were a refined, pale blue.

At bedtime Valpy was subdued, and when Penelope tucked him in he did something unusual. He asked for a good-night kiss. She immediately gave him one on his forehead.

"Today was Tina's birthday," he said.

"I know."

"You didn't say anything."

"I'm sorry, Valpy. I was waiting for you to say something."

"I drew her a picture."

"Let me see it."

He pulled his notebook out from under the covers and opened it. "Two, actually. I don't know which one to give her." Like Penelope, he had a tendency to put his drawings inside a snug frame. The first was a donkey with bells on its halter; the other was a view of mountains. "Those are the ones we can see from our window. I memorized them. Round, round, peaked, jagged, round."

"Oh, Valpy. I like them both very much," Penelope said.

·· *Truth* ··

Doña Elena asserted that Valpy had overwatered the poinsettias. "The saucers are full, and the leaves are turning yellow. Water is splashed all over the floor!" A group went to examine the evidence, and when this did not appear to be true, she said Chela must have already mopped it up.

Chela burned the tortillas for the first time in twenty-five years. A robin began singing at night. Elena demanded to know if it was true that Valpy had swept the front hall past sundown?

"Who told you, Doña?" Chela asked.

"Mrs. Slater."

All through Mirando there was a curious atmosphere of expecting the worst, and the next day Jasper disappeared from his cage and Pax had a limp. Valpy offered to call for Jasper until he came back, but Elena refused. She said there was nothing he could do.

Then Tuesday, January 27, Penelope was summoned to the

drawing room at two o'clock, far ahead of the day visitors. She had been at Mirando for eighty-seven days. She found the Doñas listening to the cantilena, Elena wrapped in the blue serape. When Penelope entered, Elena pointed to where she should sit. She was not drunk yet, though Doña Anita was well on her way.

"It is so beautiful," Doña Elena said about the cantilena. "I hate that it is about a cloud in the sky." She listened a moment longer, then lifted the needle. "Mrs. Fitzgerald, you and I share something, I believe." Elena sat and folded her hands in her lap, a smile on her face, her festive pessimism on full display. A bad sign, Penelope knew. She folded her hands to match the Doña's.

"Our lives have been saddled with the weak. You seem to have a hopeless husband. I have my sister-in-law."

Anita stirred and frowned.

Elena turned to her side table, moved some papers, and revealed Penelope's red notebook. It was lying open to pages thick with handwriting. "I want to like people. I really do. But they invariably disappoint me. Esperanza found this when she was helping with the laundry. I asked her to go into the rooms to collect the bedsheets for washing. It wasn't the usual day, I admit, but everything has been off since Chela's absence."

"Yes, I agree."

The Doña nodded. "Esperanza was moving quickly and did not see from which room the book came. Fortunately Mrs. Slater happened by and she brought it to me. We've all been so curious about your writing."

"I don't keep my notebooks in my bedsheets," Penelope said.

"Nevertheless."

Doña Elena opened the notebook and began to read aloud. "'None of the native inhabitants of Fonseca saved any money and this was a moral imperative.' Is this a story?"

"It is fiction, yes. Have you read all of it?"

"Several times." The Doña flipped ahead a few pages. "I have one or two questions. This slapping of the tortillas. You have spoken with Mrs. Clancy, I presume."

"I have."

"And you gained over the course of those conversations a sense of the way she approaches her educational outreach? She is an expert in the field, a leading member of our community." She stared at Penelope.

"I know."

Doña Elena looked down again. "This child, Lucy."

"Yes."

The silence went on for several minutes. Pax sauntered in, circled Penelope's ankles, then the Doña's ankles, then sat in a patch of sun on the floor by the windows and began to bathe. Finally the Doña spoke. "There was a fire, but Lucy didn't die in it."

Penelope did not think it would be helpful to say the word "fiction" again.

"She died in childbirth. She was twenty-six."

"Lucy had a child?" said Penelope.

Chela stifled a sob.

"Sorry, who is Lucy?" asked the Delaney. He had been summoned too.

Elena smiled. "I'm surprised you don't know, Mr. Delaney. My younger sister, of course. She had a daughter who died of fever when she was little."

Chela stifled another sob.

The room was quiet while the Doña read on. "This sentence," she said. "'I have been here sixty-six years and still feel that I am no more than a guest in this country.' I said something like that. I think I said it the night you arrived when I invited you to add something to our ofrenda." Doña Elena began turning the pages quickly. "So is this a story or not? Is this true or not?"

Penelope took a deep breath. "Fiction is not the truth, but there is truth in it." She did not expect this to help.

"You gave us a family motto or curse, something vaguely magical. 'Always Watching.'"

"I might change that."

Elena dropped her hands to her lap. "Who do you think you are? You're not good enough to have magic in your story."

"I agree."

Doña Elena shut the notebook with a slap. "This is my home. I've been here all my life. I invited you." Her voice was rising.

Doña Anita opened her eyes and sat up straight. "Now, now. Little birds in their nest agree."

Elena scoffed with an unpleasant noise from the back of her throat. "That is demonstrably wrong. Baby birds fight for every last scrap their mother brings and sometimes push the weakling out of the nest."

Valpy looked up at Penelope. "Why did you have to write a

story? Why couldn't you make it true?" He was fighting back tears with all the dignity he had.

Elena held out the notebook. "You may have this back, but it is time for you both to leave."

The Delaney tried to speak, but the Doña held up a hand. "You," she said. "I will talk to you tomorrow."

CHELA SAID SHE could not understand why Esperanza had not given the notebook to her. "She is my cousin's wife's sister's daughter and I love her, but I curse her for such nosiness! Why didn't she bring it to me?"

"It's not her fault," Penelope said. "Violet Slater found it."

"But why did she wash the sheets on a Thursday?"

"Because you were not here," Penelope said. "That is the day Violet Slater comes and Mirando is shown." Both were surprised at how much this sounded like Chela.

The next day the oven door broke, and the flock of mourning doves left the roof. "They have gone to find a house where guests do not abuse their hosts," Doña Anita said.

Mr. Whishaw arrived in the afternoon to discuss the state of Mr. Azuela's estate, which was not good. "Not good at all," he said.

"Of course, there is a fine line between financial health and insolvency," Doña Anita said. Doña Elena laughed. Both had been drinking since noon.

"No, there isn't!" cried Mr. Whishaw. "A wide margin between the two should be the very definition of financial health. This is what I am always trying to say."

It could not be helped that Valpy's birthday was two days later, January 30. Mirando was quiet and subdued. Jesús made a piñata—the traditional star shape with a point for each of the seven deadly sins, though he told Valpy the seven points were for his age. No one had the strength to think about sin. Jesús intended to fill it with pretty wrapped candy from the supermercado, but the week's events had left him no time for shopping. Chela said it was a shame—Valpy deserved better—but she had nothing in her kitchen except some pieces of sugar cane. They filled the piñata together, then watched, along with the Delaney and Mr. Flatley, as Valpy was blindfolded and given a broomstick. He swung well and broke it open in fewer than a dozen strikes. If he was disappointed by the contents, Chela's churro cake and champurrado more than made up for it. Penelope gave him one of the wise men for his growing nativity collection (the one carrying frankincense); the Delaney gave him a little sheep to go with his donkey. Valpy asked if Pax could have a treat, and Chela gave him a dish of cream, and that was the end of the festivities.

Suddenly Valpy said, "Will Mr. Azuela be here tonight? He promised to bring me a piece of ore from the mine."

No one knew what to say. A sob rose in Penelope's throat so suddenly it couldn't be stopped.

"Penelope!" the Delaney cried.

The rest of them didn't know which was more surprising: the very composed Englishwoman suddenly crying or the fact that she and the Delaney were on a first-name basis. No one knew what to say. No one wanted Valpy to know Doña Elena was telling everyone he had swept after sunset the very stairs where Mr. Azuela had fallen.

After the party, such as it was, the afternoon shadows were long. "Look," Valpy said, pointing to his shadow in the garden. "I'm bigger already. Is that why you're sad, Mama?"

"Let me see," Penelope said, and came to stand beside him.

THAT NIGHT PENELOPE did not go to the drawing room. She left Mirando, heading across the square in the golden but chilly light. Halfway across she was startled by a woman working in one of the garden beds. Like a ghost, the woman seemed to rise up out of the bed itself, her coat the same burgundy as the mounds of flowers around her, a knit hat on her head against the cold. She couldn't have been more than five feet tall.

"Buenas noches." She smiled, stretching her back.

"It is not," Penelope said, but the woman must not have understood because she kept smiling. "Hermosas flores," Penelope said.

The woman nodded. "La gracia de las flores," she said, then leaned over and disappeared back into the bed.

At El Dublín, Penelope ordered a glass of champagne. Why not? She understood why Desmond drank—of course she did. Alcohol was a way of absorbing your past. We drink our ghosts. Put another way: to be sober was to be in balance between past and present, but balance was not always possible. Sometimes it was impossible. She drank the whole glass.

They would leave Fonseca, she decided, as soon as possible. And despite all Chela's warnings, they would go back on the long-distance bus to New York. They had no other choice. That she was leaving knowing what it felt like to be hated, she attributed to forces beyond her control and hoped only that Valpy had been spared.

The next morning Ernest was gone. He left early, even before the windows rattled. Chela was sorry not to send him with food for the road. But which road? Where did he go? Penelope didn't believe he was from New York or New Jersey. Rumor circulated. Why had he left so suddenly? Had he upset the Doñas? Was he really a Delaney? Had he really called Mrs. Fitzgerald by her first name? He was so talented and charming, but many felt he had been hiding some sorrow. And who isn't?

Penelope would remember the Delaney as a kind and beautiful man who had smelled of soap and linen and heat and happiness. She was sorry they had not had a chance to say goodbye. Under the once-blue door he had slipped a postcard. On the front was an aerial view of the lake the shape of Mexico. On the back he'd written, "Penelope, exits are the most difficult part of life. I will never forget Fonseca. Ernest"

On the last day, with the last of her money, she bought herself a serape at the mercado. She'd hoped to find another blue one, but the only one she could afford was red.

# FEBRUARY

Dear ——

Some loose ends:

The only photo we have from the trip is of me in the garden in my sombrero.

I do not recall PM talking to me about our trip to Mexico in later life, even though I went several times for academic purposes and took my family there for several months in 1979. Also, Mexico does not feature in her novels even though she wrote articles on Mexican art after we returned from Saltillo.

None the less, I did eventually become a professor of economic development and an expert on Latin America. My biographer attributes this in part to this childhood exposure to poverty in Mexico.

Finally, we left for New York. I recall that we went by aeroplane (an enormous "silver" one) from Mexico City airport. Then on RMS *Franconia*, much smaller and less luxurious, back to Liverpool and London.

Regarding the fate of my mother's serape: PM was upset about Tina using it as a carpet because it was one of the very few things rescued from the sinking of the *Grace*. PM had used it as a bedspread and was fond of it, but serapes are very tough and widely used as rugs in Mexico and Texas.

Best wishes,<br>
Valpy

## ·· Candlemas ··

They left on Monday, February 2, Candlemas, midpoint between winter and spring, celebration of light and prosperity. Chela was packing up Mirando's nacimiento, carefully wrapping the holy infant for his annual blessing at San Esteban, but she allowed Valpy to pick one figure to take home with him as a souvenir. He chose a revolutionary and then turned to Pax. "Will he remember me?"

"Of course," Chela said. But because Chela never lied, she wasn't very good at it.

"The question is, will you remember him?" she said, trying to cover the error, her throat tight from trying not to cry.

Valpy buried his face in the warm black fur, and Chela put her hand on the back of his head, closed her eyes for a blessing, and tucked a piece of paper into his little hand. Then she turned away and packed up the rest of the nacimiento so roughly she nearly snapped a leg off a camel. She would normally prepare a feast of pancakes for the Candlemas evening meal, but she didn't think anything would feel normal again for some time.

Jesús drove them to the station. The bus was on time, and after a brief stop in Monterrey, they headed north toward Laredo. As they crossed the Rio Grande, Penelope wrote back to Ernest.

"Valpy is beside me learning the Lord's Prayer in Spanish. Chela wrote it out for him before we left. I've always loved it, thought it so simple and irrefutably complete. After all it's the only place in the Bible where we're told exactly how to pray. And yet after Fonseca I see it needs an edit. We need another verb. There's something missing before that bit about temptation:

> *Our Father, who art in heaven,*
> *hallowed be thy Name,*
> *thy kingdom come,*
> *thy will be done,*
> *on earth as it is in heaven.*
> *Give us this day our daily bread,*
> *and forgive us our trespasses,*
> *as we forgive those*
> *who trespass against us.*
>
> *?*
>
> *And lead us not into temptation,*
> *but deliver us from evil.*
> *For thine is the kingdom,*
> *and the power, and the glory,*
> *for ever and ever. Amen.*

"What should we add?

- *Accommodate our flaws*
- *Comfort our turmoil*
- *Succor our wounds*
- *Reveal our courage*
- *Review our strengths*
- *Remind us of joy*

"Which would you have, Ernest? You pick. Any one of them would be an improvement, the extra solace inestimable. Don't you agree?"

THE REST OF THE JOURNEY had no incidents, detours, or delays. She never mailed the letter, of course. It was in her notebook, and she did not have an address for him anyway.

After *World Review* folded and Chestnut Lodge was abandoned, she would remember her last glimpse of the blue-tinged mountains, farther than they seemed. In Southwold, the place she perched briefly with the children while Desmond tried to resume his law career, she would look across the cold, bleak shoreline, watch the wheeling flocks of terns, and recall the warmth and possibility that was Fonseca. At the end of the long watery vistas, it certainly looked like the sea met the sky. One morning she saw a heron high above the estuary with an eel half-in, half-out of its gullet, and she thought of Mirando. In fact, she would always think of Mirando whenever she dreamed too big.

She and Valpy stayed one night in New York City. After dinner in the cheap hotel, he ordered a hot chocolate. When it arrived he smelled it, tasted it, then pushed the mug away.

"I'll try to make it when we're home," Penelope said.

Valpy didn't say anything. They both knew it wouldn't be the same.

They boarded the *Franconia*, third class, the next morning and sailed for England. Penelope knew then that if she ever wrote a novel about a wife leaving, it would begin with the cost of the trip.

"Do you regret going?" It was the bank manager again, sounding very dour.

"To Fonseca? No. Anyway, Fonseca wasn't a place. It didn't have a latitude and longitude. If anything it was an idea, or a time. It was a dry well. It was certainly the end of a dream and the beginning of a long wait."

"You must be joking."

"I'm not. I suppose I'd feel differently if there'd been a villain, but there wasn't."

"Really? In Fonseca you fell in love, played a role in a death, betrayed a friend, disappointed your son, and compromised your deepest family values."

"Are you suggesting I am the villain?"

"I'm suggesting you were at least sand in the gears."

Penelope thought this was probably true. "Money is to blame. And possibly Mrs. Slater." She retracted this. "No. Part of me pities Violet Slater. She wanted more children."

"Should pity be subdivided?" the bank manager asked.

"Good point," she conceded.

"If things had gone differently in Fonseca, you might have been as rich as a lord. You would have had the money to keep *World Review* running; Desmond would not have had to return so disastrously to the law. You would not have had to live on a sinking houseboat!"

It was hard to hold the center after *Grace* sank, it's true. She will concede this to herself and herself only. "It was not meant to be," she said angrily. "I attempted something for which I was never equipped. I didn't know how to get a legacy. I still don't."

"Would you agree it was a treasure hunt that became a mystery that turned into a love story?"

"I believe Fonseca cannot be explained."

"But you failed."

She had indeed. She was embarrassed and ashamed.

"Are you worried about your family's future?"

Yes, of course, and yet she truly believed it would sort itself out. She believed, in general, that everything went wrong and was disappointing, but you continued, for what was the alternative?

"Experiences aren't given us to be got over; otherwise they would hardly be experiences. Courage and endurance are useless if they are never tested."

"You're all set then," the bank manager said.

She'd been in Fonseca ninety-one days. Her memory of it would always be clear and sharp and fierce and abiding. She would keep a love of red notebooks and salmon poinsettias, blue rooms and black cats, roses and camellias. She would love pealing church bells and the sound of the requinto. She would appreciate a good package tour when traveling abroad and never again wear silver. Fonseca changed her, but the story of the legacy belonged to the world of *what-if*—fiction. When the *Franconia* arrived in Liverpool, she was back in the real world, the very real world, of *what now?*

First, Tina was collected from her mother-in-law. Penelope arrived at the end of Tina's nap, and mother and daughter sat on the bed watching each other for a long time. Penelope found it hard to reintroduce herself. Tina had changed more than she'd thought possible. Eventually Tina slid off the bed to retrieve a book she'd been given for her birthday. She did not give it to her mother for a reading, only showed it to her from afar. Penelope admired it and wished she could have shown her the Caballito. But along with a few other coins, Penelope had put it in the lamb bank, knowing that Valpy would never break it open. As promised, he did give the bank to Tina, and she accepted it gravely, cautiously, touching the long wolfish snout with the tip of a finger. For two months Tina spoke to Penelope only in a whisper.

*World Review* closed with its April–May 1953 issue, a special Mexico edition almost entirely devoted to her essay on Mexican art, "From the Golden Land: A Study of Mexican Art and History." She thought she might have the story ready, too, but she didn't, so they ran one by Norman Mailer, "Pierrot," that they'd been holding for a while.

Penelope wrote the note that appeared at the front.

*This is the last issue of* World Review *in its present form. For a* number of reasons, already familiar to most of us, we have had to suspend publication. We hope, however, after an interval, World Review will appear again in a new form and devoted entirely to literature.

Maria was born healthy and strong on April 10, 1953. She became a celebrated neurobiologist, a world leader in the science of pain in infants and children, and how early experience of pain—even in utero—can shape pain sensitivity for life.

That summer Penelope received a letter from Jo. It wasn't very long and contained a lot of news of Edward. Apparently they had found success in Guanajuato after Fonseca, and Jo wished Penelope could see some of the work Edward had done there. They were back in New York, and all was well. At the end she thanked Penelope again for the drawing she'd given her.

"It means a great deal to me and I keep it near. Do you know the poem 'Waiting' by John Burroughs? I like the first stanza: 'Serene I fold my hands and wait, Nor care for wind, nor tide, nor sea; I rave no more 'gainst time or fate, For lo! My own shall come to me.'" She signed off, "Cheerily, Jo." But in the end waiting didn't serve her. In 1967, Edward died, Jo the year after that. The Whitney Museum, to which Jo bequeathed all their work, kept Edward's paintings and discarded all but three of Jo's.

Penelope never found the reality of poverty worse than she'd expected, but the rest of the family was surprised. She kept them all going through the worst of their shelter and council-flat years. "Borracho" became "bonky"—the children's word for their father when he was drunk—and somewhere Valpy began to drift away. He separated himself from the household chaos and even his early literary and artistic leanings. Fonseca had changed him too.

Penelope tried many times to write the Mexico novel, and she might have kept trying, but the red notebook, along with so much else, was lost when the *Grace* went down. It continued to be her habit, however, to turn notebooks upside down and use them back to front for writing fiction, and in this way she finished "Our Lives Are Only Lent to Us" and submitted it to the *Blackwood's Magazine* short-story contest. It didn't win and she put it away. But for the rest of her life she would remember Genaro's hurt, Azuela's hope, Jo's predicament, Reynoso's dignity, Chela's strength. She was sorry not to put them in a novel. She tried to forget the duplicity of the Violet Slaters of the world, but as they were essentially everywhere, the effort felt pointless. Much later she learned that Mirando had become the Delaney House Art and Cultural Center. Violet Slater and Rose Clancy must have both won and shared the spoils.

Just before sleep—never again in a proper bed, always preferring sofas and other transitional pieces—Penelope often thought of Ernest. She hoped he was fine. She hoped he wasn't dreaming alone. Her dreams were sometimes full of him, and they were good, wonderful, even embarrassing dreams. They were filled with the fragrances, sights, and sounds of Fonseca, and the flavors of Chela's cooking. If she chanced to hear "Mar y cielo" in later years, which was more often than she anticipated due to the rising international popularity of the Trío Los Panchos, she had to exit the store or café or wherever she was as soon as possible. "Que nunca, nunca, nunca el mar lo alcanzará." The yearning in the repeated nevers could stop her breath. In the end, though, she always took the bus, crossed the ocean, boarded the train, and stepped up the front walk of Chestnut Lodge.

The gate was fixed. Desmond had seen to it.

"Do you think he will be making tea?" Valpy asked. They were standing before the front door.

Penelope took his hand and squeezed it. "I will do it." She looked down at him. "You know there is no money, Valpy?"

"We went a long way to be told that," he said.

"I imagine we'll remember it." She opened the door and walked into the house.

As for the Lord's Prayer, it remains the same as it ever was, not quite powerful enough for all it is asked to do.

Dear ——

I was so pleased to hear from you as I had been wondering how you were getting on. Forgive my slow reply but I am just getting over a nasty bout of pleurisy and like you my life is full of responsibilities and arrangements and holding everything together as far as possible.

I feel every confidence that the book will complete itself and it is a pleasure in store for the future.

You might like to know that the local arts society have put a plaque up on 25 Almeric Rd in London where she lived with me and my husband and wrote many of her books. It was a very strange occasion standing outside the house where we had lived when we were so young and where my father died and listening to tributes and speeches. I will send you a photo.

Keep in touch won't you?

>Meanwhile best wishes from rainswept Cornwall,
>Tina

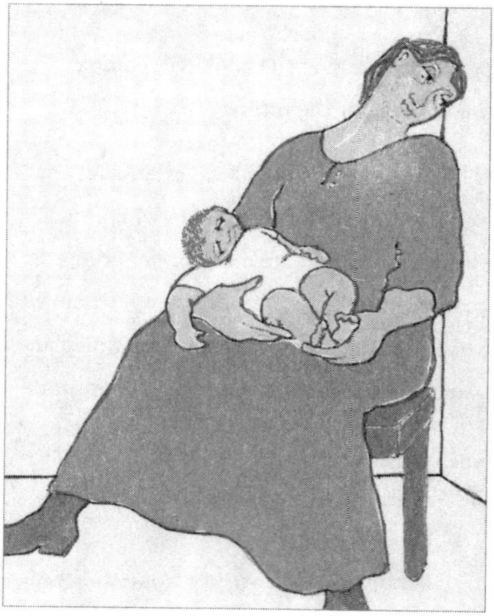

*Author's Note*

Penelope Fitzgerald published her first novel in 1977 when she was sixty years old. She went on to write eight more before she died in 2000. Her work was widely read and critically acclaimed, but in the decades before her literary success, Fitzgerald and her family faced severe financial hardship and uncertainty. This novel is based on a journey she made to northern Mexico in 1952 as the family descended into poverty. Uncharacteristically, Fitzgerald left almost no record or fictional account of this time. Friends and family members didn't know why she went to Mexico, and she never spoke of it after she returned. But in 1980 she wrote an essay titled "Following the Plot" in which she seems to set the scene.

"Suppose I were to try to write a story which began with a journey I made to the north of Mexico twenty-seven years ago, taking with me my son, then aged five. We were going to pay a winter visit to two old ladies called Delaney who lived comfortably, in spite of recent economic reforms, on the proceeds of the family silver mine." She describes the house, "a shuttered mansion in the French style," says the sisters suggested they were looking for an heir, and reveals that after she arrived, "everyone in Fonseca who was interested in the Delaneys' wealth . . . wanted to get rid of me and my son as soon as possible."

"If I got as far as this," she writes, "I should have to stop. The details are accurate, these things happened in Fonseca, and many more were to follow."

But Fonseca does not exist. The town she visited in Mexico was Saltillo, the name Fonseca perhaps a rueful invention, as in Latin it means "dry well." So are we in a real or an imagined place? A little later in the essay, she writes that she was sorry to let the story go because of what she considered the natural energy of the plot. She felt she didn't have "the capacity to relate the wide-spreading complications of the Mexican legacy, however well I remembered them."

I discovered Fitzgerald's work in 1999. My husband and I had just moved to London for his job, and I, homesick in a rental flat near Battersea, was at sea. On his way home from work one day, Mitchell stopped in a bookshop, and that night he gave me a copy of Fitzgerald's novel *Offshore*. Neither of us had heard of the author, but he thought I might like it because it was set along the Thames near where we were living. I read all her other novels in short order. She

Author's Note · 253

was living in Hampstead then, and I dreamed I might meet her somehow. I never did, but her work has been a touchstone for me ever since.

The relationship between history, biography, and fiction interested Fitzgerald. It interests me too. Seven years ago I decided to use all three to try to write the story of the Mexico trip. Among other things, I discovered the Hoppers traveled to Saltillo three times to paint and were there the same winter Fitzgerald was. Whether the three met, however, is unknown.

After this novel was announced, Fitzgerald's literary executor, her son-in-law Terence Dooley, contacted me to say the family was interested and wanted to be in touch. That fall of 2020 I began a correspondence with her son, Valpy, and her daughter Tina. I treasure their emails, which were written in response to my questions, and am greatly indebted to them for allowing me to include extracts from them in the book.

As I worked, I took Fitzgerald's "Following the Plot" as a guide, specifically a few lines that I read as clues: "Everyone has a point to which the mind reverts naturally when it is left on its own." I believe the Mexico trip was that point for her.

"We left on the long-distance bus without a legacy, but knowing what it was to be hated." "Hated" is a strong word for her to use. In her novels, she is a master of understatement, always.

And finally, "Unfortunate are the events that are never narrated," which I have used as an epigraph. She put it in quotation marks, but her family and I have been unable to figure out what she was quoting. Possibly she invented it, just as she invented the epigraph she used in *The Blue Flower*, "Novels arise out of the shortcomings of history."

*Acknowledgments*

Many people, places, books, and paintings helped me write this novel, but I must begin with Penelope Fitzgerald's own work. I've been reading and rereading her novels, short stories, reviews, essays, and biographies for twenty-six years.

Other sources that helped inform my story of Fitzgerald and this time in her life include: *Penelope Fitzgerald: A Life* by Hermione Lee; *So I Have Thought of You: The Letters of Penelope Fitzgerald*, edited by Terence Dooley; *The Afterlife: Essays and Criticism*, edited by Terence Dooley, Christopher Carduff, and Mandy Kirkby; *Penelope Fitzgerald* by Hugh Adlington; *Collected Ghost Stories* by M. R. James (Oxford World's Classics); *The Seven Lamps of Architecture* by John Ruskin; "Penelope Fitzgerald's Unknown Fiction" by Dean Fowler and Linda Henchey (*The Hudson Review* 61, no. 1, spring 2008); "The Peripatetic Penelope Fitzgerald" by Lucy Scholes (*Granta*, July 2017); *LRB Selections 2: Penelope Fitzgerald* (with introduction by Hermione Lee); *Saltillo*

*1770–1810: Town and Region in the Mexican North* by Leslie S. Offutt; and *Baedeker's Mexico*.

I found *Edward Hopper: An Intimate Biography* by Gail Levin and *Edward Hopper: The Watercolors* by Virginia M. Mecklenburg instrumental in guiding my understanding of the Hoppers and their travels in Mexico.

I am grateful to Alejandro Leal-Pulido at the Metropolitan Museum of Art and Suzanne Greenawalt at the Yale University Art Gallery for making the arrangements necessary for me to see Edward Hopper's Saltillo watercolors not on view. These include *Saltillo Mansion* (brilliantly used on the jacket of this book by Darren Haggar) and *Church of San Esteban* at the Met and *Mountains of Guanajuato* at the Yale Art Gallery.

I'd like to thank the Harry Ransom Center, the Vartan Gregorian Center for Research in the Humanities at the New York Public Library, and Millay Arts for work space, research assistance, and inspiration.

To my dear early readers—Clare Aronow, Rachel Cohen, Olivia Kane, Fiona McCrae, Janice Nimura, Laurie Nutt, and Oscar Villalon—thank you for your insights. Each of you made the book better.

To my treasured agent and editor—PJ Mark and Ginny Smith—you waited a long time for this one and kept my spirits up along the way. Thank you for your expert advice and enthusiasm through it all. Thanks also to Caroline Sydney for working so hard to get everything just right, especially the art in this book and the last one.

Penelope Fitzgerald's family has been supportive of this novel from the beginning, an immeasurable gift. My greatest hope is that people will read *Fonseca* and then want to read all of Fitzgerald's books. Start with any of them. My favorite is *The Beginning of Spring*. Thank you, Edmund Valpy Fitzgerald and Christina and Terence Dooley for believing in me and this project.

*Fonseca* is dedicated to Mitchell, best friend, husband, everything. He put Penelope Fitzgerald's *Offshore* in my hands when I needed it most. I also want to include Michael Downing, brilliant writer and friend, whose voice I will always hear when I write.